Murder
Passes
The Buck

FORTHCOMING BY DEB BAKER

Murder Grins & Bears It

Murder
Passes
The Buck

Deb Baker

MIDNIGHT INK
WOODBURY, MINNESOTA

First Edition
First Printing, 2006

Book design by Donna Burch
Cover design by Lisa Novak
Cover illustration © 2006 by Cathy Gendron
Editing by Connie Hill

Midnight Ink, an imprint of Llewellyn Publications

Library of Congress Cataloging-in-Publication Data

Baker, Deb (Debra), 1953–
    Murder passes the buck : a Yooper mystery / Deb Baker. — 1st ed.
       p.   cm.
    ISBN-13: 978-0-7387-0872-0
    ISBN-10: 0-7387-0872-0
       1. Michigan—Fiction.   I. Title.

PS3602.A586M87   2006
813'.6—dc22   2006044990

Midnight Ink
Llewellyn Publications
2143 Wooddale Drive, Dept. 0-7387-0872-0
Woodbury, MN 55125-2989, U.S.A.
www.midnightinkbooks.com

Printed in the United States of America

ONE

Word for the Day
INCHOATE (in KOH it) adj.
Not yet clearly or completely formed;
in the early stages.

IF MY GRANDSON, LITTLE Donny, hadn't taken so long getting out of bed this morning, I would have been at Chester's hunting blind in time to see them haul Chester out. I've never seen a bullet hole smack in the middle of someone's head before.

Instead, I sat in the passenger seat of Barney's white Ford pickup truck with my twelve-gauge shotgun at my feet and a box of buckshot in my lap. I laid on the horn until all two hundred and fifty pounds of six-foot-four Little Donny shuffled out and stuffed himself into the driver's seat. He was clutching a chicken salad sandwich in one hand and tucking his shirt in with the other.

It's times like these I wish I'd learned to drive. Up until Barney passed on, I didn't need to. He took me wherever I wanted to go. Now I'm at the mercy of slugs, and I don't mean the bullet kind.

Little Donny is nineteen years old, and he really appreciates the backwoods. He came to the Michigan Upper Peninsula, the U.P., as we call it, from his home in Milwaukee the day before yesterday for the opening of deer-hunting season, which is today, November fifteenth. At the first gray streak of daylight you could hear rifles going off all over the woods, and that's when Chester got it right between the eyes.

"I suppose I missed the whole thing," I called out the window when we pulled up outside of Chester's blind.

My son, Blaze, leaned against his rust-bucket yellow pickup with SHERIFF printed on the side, filling out paperwork. No one else was around. Either we'd beat the ambulance or it had already transported its patient.

"Just finishing up," he muttered, still writing in his notebook, not noticing my disappointment. "Chester's body is at the morgue in Escabana by now. How did you find out about it?"

"Heard it on the scanner."

Last year when Barney died, I cold-packed my dreams in a canning jar and placed them high on a dusty shelf in my pantry. A week after I buried him I turned sixty-six and Cora Mae bought me a police scanner for my birthday. It sat in my closet until three days ago when I mentioned to someone that I'm a recent widow and Cora Mae let me have it. "Gertie Johnson, I know you loved Barney, but it's time to start living again. Let's go over to your house and listen to that scanner I gave you. Maybe something will pop up."

Something had popped up, and that something had popped Chester.

I jumped down from the cab and the box of buckshot fell to the ground.

"That thing better not be loaded," Blaze said, after heaving himself off the truck and glancing at the shotgun on the floor. "You know it's against the law to transport a loaded weapon in a vehicle. We've been through this before."

"Of course it's not loaded," I lied, picking up the box of buckshot and stuffing it under the seat.

Little Donny crawled out of the driver's seat, and I couldn't help noticing a glob of mustard stuck on his chin. And I couldn't help noticing that Blaze couldn't button the bottom of his sheriff's uniform shirt anymore.

I sighed, thinking of Chester's family and how they'd feel when they heard the bad news, and for a few minutes Little Donny's sloppiness and Blaze's escalating weight gain didn't seem important at all.

"What happened here?" I asked.

"Nothing much to it," Blaze said, shaking his head. "Stray bullet whomped into the blind and caught poor unlucky Chester right between the eyes. We have at least one shooting accident every hunting season."

The air was clean and crisp, and Blaze's breath steamed around his head while he talked. I could smell cheap cologne hanging in the air. Blaze always wore too much.

"Remember last year," he continued, "that guy in Trenary was shot in the stomach sleeping in bed. Remember that, Little Donny?"

"Yeah, I remember."

"So you're writing this off as an accident?" I stammered, in disbelief.

Blaze looked surprised that I would even suggest anything else. "It was an accident and don't go saying anything different."

Ever since Blaze turned forty-four all he thinks about is retirement, even though he still has a few years left if he wants a full pension. He's already retired in his mind and that's the scary thing. He doesn't care anymore and is just putting in his time. Maybe he needs me to watch out for him, make him walk the straight and narrow. Maybe I have to be tough with him.

"What if someone murdered Chester and you're letting a killer get away with it?" I pulled off my Blue Blocker sunglasses so he could see my glare. "I bet that's what happened, and you're too lazy to follow through with a proper investigation."

"Ma, quit. I really hate to disappoint you, but nobody ever gets murdered in Stonely. You've been watching too many soap operas again."

"I've never watched a soap opera in my life. But I have some inchoate ideas about this."

"Inchoate ideas?"

"It's my word for the day."

Last week I decided it was time for some self-improvement. I'm expanding my vocabulary by learning one new word every day and I have to use it in normal conversation so it sticks with me. I've found it's best to try out my new word first thing in the morning or else I forget to use it.

"Who found Chester?" I wanted to know.

"Floy . . ." Blaze hesitated and shook his head. "Oh, no. I'm not telling you right now. You'll just go over and bother the poor man. He's upset enough as it is."

"Well, stop by on your way home later and let me know what's happening."

Blaze lives in a mobile home on the east forty. Barney and I—well, just me now—own three forties, meaning I own one hundred and twenty acres. The properties in Tamarack Township are sectioned in blocks of forty acres so when someone asks how much land you own, you say two forties, or five forties, or whatever.

The terrain in the Upper Peninsula is as rugged and as difficult to categorize as the people who settled here—miles and miles of swampy lowlands, then miles of even country with every type of pine tree you can imagine, and when you think you have it all figured out, the elevation soars and you find yourself high on a wind-blown ridge overlooking one of the Great Lakes, watching waves slam against enormous rocks.

Most of us own a lot of land and we're proud of it, even though it comes cheap. It's all we have.

Blaze lives on the east forty with his wife, Mary. His two girls are off at college. My youngest daughter, Star, lives in a log cabin on the west forty. Her kids are grown and gone and her no-good husband left her for a blonde bimbo, so she's there alone. But her kids visit often.

Heather is Little Donny's mother. She, her husband, Big Donny, and Little Donny, my favorite grandson and current chauffeur, live in Milwaukee.

I like the fact that two of my kids stayed in Stonely and decided to live on the family property. I like the fact that they have to drive right past my house coming and going. Sometimes it's stressful having family right on top of me, but in the final analysis, it's worth it.

"Let's go hunting later, Blaze," Little Donny said.

"Stop calling me Blaze," Blaze said, glaring at me while prying open the door of his rust-bucket truck. "I legally changed my name to Brian. I keep telling everyone in town over and over, and no one can seem to get it straight."

"Brian?" Little Donny was confused, which isn't anything new for him.

"You weren't born a Brian and you don't look like a Brian," I huffed. "Who's going to call you that? It's not your real name."

"Your Granny, here," Blaze said to Little Donny, ignoring me except for an accusing finger pointed in my direction, "named me after a horse."

Which was true.

———

I wanted to look around the crime scene, but Blaze wouldn't let me. He waited in his dump truck—as in what-a-dump truck—until we pulled out ahead of him. At my direction, Little Donny turned right on Highway M35. I knew Blaze would turn left and head toward town, and I didn't want him following us all the way back.

He had a family to inform of their loss. I had a crime scene to investigate.

"Nice and slow," I cautioned Little Donny. I wore a blaze orange hunting jacket, since those crazy hunters will shoot at anything moving. I had my hair pulled up under an orange hunting cap with the earflaps folded up. Two trucks passed us going the opposite way, the drivers also wearing hunter's orange. I waved and they waved back.

As soon as Blaze turned left, I slapped Little Donny's knee. "Turn around and head back to Chester's."

"Blaze is going to be hot, and anyway, I want to go hunting," Little Donny crabbed.

I gave him a stern look, and he swung around at the first crossroad.

Chester's hunting blind stood on the edge of a small clearing, butting up against a grove of tamarack trees. It wasn't wrapped in yellow tape to mark it as a crime scene, confirming my suspicions that Blaze wouldn't even do a cursory investigation.

I carefully opened the blind door with the sleeve of my jacket so I wouldn't leave prints, in spite of my belief that this was one case where it wouldn't matter. I suspected there weren't any prints to find. This was a long-distance murder.

Granted, I had no evidence that Chester's death actually was a murder, but every time a stray bullet from a high-powered rifle took a life, I thought about whether it was an accident or not. In the Michigan U.P., it would be the perfect crime.

Opening the door, I wondered who or what Chester might have seen before he died.

The shack was built on a movable platform so it could be towed around on the back of a tractor. We all did that. One reason is that it's nice and easy to move next season if we find a better hunting spot, and another reason is so the federal government can't slap a tax on us for building a permanent structure. They try to get you coming and going.

Inside, I could feel the leftover warmth of the propane heater as I looked around.

Chester's blind was pretty ordinary, built for comfort, warmth, and an unobstructed shot when Big Buck strolled out into the clearing. It had an insulated wood frame and windows on each side, the same as a house. Metal fasteners on the sides of the windows could be turned, and the window would silently swing out. The floor was covered with worn brown shag carpet. A can of WD40 was in the corner along with a cooler full of beer, a can of peanuts, and a pair of binoculars.

Even though I considered Chester a neighbor, I didn't know him real well. He kept to himself out on Parker Road, nodding his head when we met, then moving on. Not a chit-chatter. His wife died a few years back, before Barney died. Everyone thought she went plumb loco until the doctors discovered the brain tumor. Then it was too late.

When I left his blind, I knew a little more about him. I knew he drank the cheapest beer he could buy, and that he drank it early in the day. He must have slammed down a few cans before he was slammed down himself by a deadly bullet. I saw several empty cans tossed in a pile on the floor. An open can on a small table had spilled and beer had run in a stream with the blood from his head.

I also learned that a hole in the head makes quite a bloody mess, and that Chester liked smut magazines. Since I never saw one before, I paged through the stack by the window.

"Granny, this isn't a good idea. Come out of there or I'm telling Blaze."

Little Donny's large bulk blocked out the light though the door. I wanted to search for clues between the shack and the creek running through Chester's property, but I'd have to get rid of Whiney first.

"Okay, let's hit it," I said, climbing into the cab.

———

Floyd Tatrow was hard of hearing, so when I stuck my head in his kitchen door, I called out nice and loud. He didn't answer. The kitchen smelled like freshly fried bacon, and the sink was full of dirty dishes soaking in sudsy water—the water was still warm to my touch.

"Floyd," I hollered. "It's Gertie Johnson. Where are you?"

I checked every room and found them all empty. Floyd kept the place spic-and-span clean even though his wife, Eva, had a stroke a year ago and was in a private nursing home in Escanaba. He still had hopes that she would come home some day, but the rest of us knew she was there for life.

Eva was a little too church-like for my taste. Her favorite phrase was "The Lord will provide." I always thought you had to provide for yourself. No one else is going to do it for you, not even the Lord, but you couldn't reason with Eva.

Years ago when Floyd lost everything but the shirt on his back at the Indian casino, I cooked up a large roast with carrots and onions, mashed ten pounds of homegrown potatoes, and dropped the meal off at their home.

"I told you the Lord would provide," Eva said to Floyd, putting the pans down on the countertop.

"That wasn't the Lord providing," I said, tapping my thumb on my chest. "That was me."

The Tatrow house was decorated in frilly yellow curtains and embroidered religious pictures. Crocheted blankets covered the upholstery and lace doilies were draped on the tables. Eva liked her arts and crafts, before the Lord provided her with a stroke that paralyzed her entire right side.

That private nursing home must be costing Floyd a pretty penny, I thought, eyeing a television set as big as my entire dining room wall. He better learn to cut back on his spending.

I let myself out and stood on the porch, scanning the property. I avoided looking at the truck where Little Donny sat fuming. Big cities squeeze the ability to be patient right out of people. Life becomes too frantic and rushed. It's a sad thing. He needed to spend more time in the woods with me, learning the art of slow and simple.

I strolled over to the sauna and yanked the door open.

There sat Floyd, naked as a blue jay and not half as pretty. He had the largest head I ever saw on a man, and was wearing a Ford baseball cap that was three sizes too small. Men around these parts don't take off their hats unless they absolutely have to.

"Gertie Johnson," Floyd exclaimed. "What are you doing?"

The difference between men and women is this—if you catch a woman butt-naked, she tries to cover the private parts with her hands. A man will sit there just like you found him even if he doesn't have much to be proud of.

Floyd sat like that, not moving.

10

"Put your drawers on," I said, looking away too late. "I'll wait outside."

Floyd took his sweet time coming out. I sat in the truck with Grumpy until Floyd opened the sauna door and walked toward the truck.

The Finns like their saunas. They usually build them around the back of the house for privacy because they roll in the snow when they're done sweating it out. Afternoon is their favorite time. It takes all morning to fire the sauna up and get it steaming hot. Sometimes a Finn will invite his friends over for a sauna, and if it's mixed company, the men go together then the women go together, and everyone tries to peek when the snow rolling begins. Especially if the moonshine has been going around.

Floyd has six or seven old geezers who share the sauna with him, and I was grateful that they weren't over today. One naked old guy is enough for any woman. I shook my head to clear the image and rolled down the truck window.

"You found Chester this morning," I said. When Blaze let it slip that Floyd found Chester, I was pretty certain he meant Floyd Tatrow. There weren't any other Floyds around Stonely.

"What?"

I remembered that Floyd couldn't hear well and repeated the question, loudly.

"It was an awful shock," he said.

"What happened?" I shouted.

"What's that?"

I looked over at Little Donny wedged into the driver's seat and our eyes met. Little Donny, who can't stay mad long, grinned at me.

11

"Is that thing turned on?" I leaned out the window and pointed at Floyd's hearing aid.

Floyd dug the hearing aid out of his ear and made an adjustment. "Sorry," he said, screwing it back in. "Blasted thing was turned off."

"What happened to Chester?"

"Shot in the head's what happened to Chester. I walked up to the blind, calling out so he wouldn't accidentally shoot me. I was going to tell him to stop over for a sauna, you see. I could tell he was past saving, but I ran back to his house and called for an ambulance anyway. Then I called the sheriff."

"What do you think happened?" I said. "In your own opinion."

Floyd leaned against the truck. "I already told you. Chester was shot in the head. That's what happened to him." He said it loud and clear like he thought I was the deaf one.

"No, I mean, do you think he was murdered?"

"Murdered! Lord, no! This is a Christian, law-abiding community, and if Chester's dead it's because God called him. When Eva could still talk she used to say 'The Lord will provide' and that's it in a nutshell, you see. God's bullet took Chester and He must have had a good reason."

Okay.

———

Cora Mae, my all-time best friend, was waiting for us at my house with a fresh pot of coffee and a plate of sweet rolls. In all the excitement, I forgot she was giving me a hair rinse today.

Cora Mae has been my friend since I moved to Stonely. I remember Barney calling Stonely "God's Country" and I'd thought he meant a paradise, like the Garden of Eden. Then we arrived and I found out it was God's Country because nobody else wanted it. No jobs worth mentioning, cracker-box houses clumped together in towns so small you missed them even though you knew you hadn't blinked, and bugs the size of pumpkins.

Cora Mae saved me. She's three years younger, making her sixty-three, and she's buried three husbands. Cora Mae never could stay away from men; they're in her blood—she's always on the lookout in spite of her bad luck in the past.

"Onni Maki's hot with the widows around here. I hear he's taking Viagra to keep up, or rather to keep it up," Cora Mae said, pouring two cups of coffee. "Sure would like to give him a whirl."

"You'll have to take a number and stand in line," I said, pulling out a kitchen chair and sitting down to tug off my hunting boots. I used to be able to take my boots off leaning against the wall, but it's been a few years now. I can do it only if I absolutely have to, using all my concentration.

I hung my hunting jacket on a peg by the door and pulled off the hunting cap, running my fingers through my short, coarse gray hair.

Little Donny took his rifle down from the gun rack, shoved a box of ammo into his jacket, and headed for the door. "Onni Maki is the only available male within fifty miles, especially since Chester's dead," he said to Cora Mae.

"What about George?" I reminded him. "George is available." I chewed my lip after realizing my mistake. Cora Mae stalks any single man who breathes air and I don't want her rushing off after

George, who is a good friend and doesn't deserve to be worked over by Cora Mae.

Glancing sideways, I saw her reading the directions on the hair product box, paying no attention to me.

"Well, good luck," Little Donny said to Cora Mae.

She peered over the top of the box and fluffed her hair with one hand. "I don't need luck, honey. I got sex appeal."

Cora Mae did look good for her age. She was wearing black stretch pants, a black long-sleeved tee, and pointy boots with two-inch heels. Her man-hunting outfit, she calls it. Last year Cora Mae discovered Wonderbras and now her boobs are always in the lead. They're the first things you notice about Cora Mae.

I must look pretty drab and nondescript next to her. Cora Mae has style. Here I am—barely five feet tall, a hundred and twenty pounds, with old-lady gray hair and a winter roll of fat around my middle that seems to increase in size every year.

I saw Little Donny heading for the door. "Where you going with my car keys?"

"Hunting with Carl. Remember? I already asked you if I could take the truck."

"Oh. Ah . . . I remember now," I said, not remembering at all.

"See you later." Little Donny slammed the door shut behind him.

"He'll be back in a minute or two," I said, chuckling. "He forgot something important."

Thirty seconds later, Donny stomped through the kitchen, opened the refrigerator, and grabbed a pile of sandwiches I'd made earlier. He had to use both pockets to stuff them all in.

"Let's get started," I said to Cora Mae after Little Donny was loaded up and gone. I clipped a towel around my neck.

Normally, I have a rinse to take the yellow out of my gray hair. Gray hair doesn't scare me. Neither do flabby muscles, or liver spots, or strange little wart-like bumps. All of which are cropping up here and there on my body like clumps of weeds. I'm slowly losing my hearing, my eyesight, and yesterday I noticed I'm losing my eyelashes. I've stopped being afraid of age since it doesn't do any good anyway. You can't stop the march of time and the sooner you accept it, the sooner you can focus on the important things in life.

Cora Mae likes to play the role of hairdresser, and although I know how to take care of my own hair, I humor her. She waved the box containing my rinse in front of my face. "You're full of surprises, Gertie."

I looked at the box and screeched. "Strawberry blonde? Oh, no. I must have picked up the wrong box."

"I think it's time for a new look," Cora Mae of the black-as-tar hair said when I attempted to grab it away. After a brief struggle, she won.

I filled her in while she worked. She knew about Chester's death because I'd called her earlier while I was waiting for Little Donny. Now I went through the graphic details.

Two hours later I stared into the mirror in disbelief and horror. My head was covered in a brassy orange mess. I grabbed the box and read the directions.

"Cora Mae, I told you it was on my head too long. It says fifteen minutes, not fifty. Now what am I going to do?"

"The clown show's coming to Escanaba. Maybe you can apply for a job." Cora Mae was holding her left side from laughing so hard, while tears streaked with mascara slid down her face. "I never saw hair take color like that before."

"Well, at least I won't need to wear my orange hunting cap." I checked my watch. "I wanted to search Chester's property but it's starting to get dark. It'll have to wait until morning."

Cora Mae had that look in her eye. The here-she-goes-again look, and I knew I was going to hear it whether I wanted to or not.

"Gertie, every time someone dies doesn't mean it's murder. Remember when Martha fell in the tub, hit her head, and drowned. You said that was murder."

"Might have been. It was poorly investigated."

"And when Ted Hakanen drove his car into the tree on the side of Peter Road, dead drunk. You said that his car had been tampered with."

"Probably was."

"Blaze sent that old Buick to Escanaba, mechanics went over it, and the only thing they found was an empty bottle of Jim Beam."

"That's what a killer would want you to believe. Maybe Martha and Ted died in accidents, but it's a numbers game, Cora Mae. One of these days it really will be murder."

We cleaned up the kitchen and polished off the bag of sweet rolls. Since I'd missed lunch, I shared a liver sausage sandwich with Cora Mae.

The thought of investigating Chester's death appealed to me. The more time I spent listening to my police scanner, the more I thought I'd make a pretty good investigator. After all, I had three kids to practice on while they were growing up. If nothing came of my efforts and it was a stray bullet that killed Chester like Blaze and Cora Mae thought, I'd chalk it up to on-the-job training.

At the moment, I knew three things. One: based on television shows I've watched, the person who finds the body sometimes turns out to be the killer. He should be the first name on a suspect list. Two: a detective has to move fast. As the murder ages, it gets harder and harder to solve. Three: Floyd Tatrow's phone number was in the telephone book.

"This is the sheriff's office calling," I said into the phone, holding my nose lightly with my fingers. "You need to take a lie detector test."

"Why would I have to do that?" Floyd wanted to know.

"It's standard procedure. You found the body, didn't you?"

"Yes, but. . . ."

"It's perfectly voluntary, of course, but you'll clear yourself right away if you agree to it."

"Clear myself of what?"

"I can't answer that. It's confidential police business. Can you be there in twenty minutes? Sheriff Johnson has the equipment at his mobile home."

"I suppose. All right, but I never heard of anything like this before."

"You never found a dead body before."

Cora Mae giggled.

"And don't eat or drink anything before the test," I finished.

"What is going through your mind?" Cora Mae asked when I hung up.

17

She's a perfect example of the difference between an investigative mind and a regular mind, if you can call Cora Mae's mind regular. Regular minds rarely have brainstorm ideas that catch killers.

I flipped on the spotlight next to the drive leading past my house to Blaze's mobile home and started gathering the supplies to make popcorn.

"If Floyd shows up, he probably didn't murder Chester," I reasoned. "The killer isn't going to willingly walk into the town sheriff's house to be hooked up to a lie detector."

I finished making the popcorn, turned off the inside lights, and waited in the dark by the window, eating popcorn. Cora Mae held the bowl. "The beauty of the whole plan," I bragged, "is that Blaze and Mary aren't home. I saw Mary drive out half an hour ago and Blaze is still working. If Floyd shows up, he'll find an empty house, take off his little cap, scratch his big head, and go on home. Blaze will never know what happened. But I'll know Floyd didn't kill Chester."

I was tossing kernels of popcorn in the air and trying to catch them in my mouth when Blaze's sheriff's truck turned onto our road and passed my house. "Oh, no," I muttered. Pretty soon Floyd's blue truck went by. When he passed under the spotlight, I could see his large, pale head peering over the dashboard.

"How are you going to explain to Blaze?" Cora Mae asked, crunching popcorn.

"I'll deny involvement," I said, disappointed that Floyd showed up. "What makes you think he'll suspect me anyway?"

Cora Mae raised one eyebrow, which isn't an easy thing to do.

A few minutes later, Floyd drove out and Cora Mae flipped the house lights on. I crossed Floyd's name off my list of suspects and stared at a blank page.

"When is Little Donny going back to Milwaukee?" Cora Mae asked.

"I don't know. He's not in any big rush, since he's between jobs."

Between jobs is what Donny calls it. I call it canned, fired, let go, but I'm not saying anything. Little Donny's had more jobs than a rabbit has bunnies.

Cora Mae picked up her purse.

"Little Donny should be back any minute," I said. "It's too dark to hunt. He must have stopped for a beer. If you wait a bit, he can drive you home."

Neither one of us drives a car, which some people from other parts of the country might consider strange, but it's not so unusual in the U.P. Things are spread out here, but we don't go out that much and when we do there's always someone willing to drive us. Once a week Blaze or his wife, Mary, drives me to the grocery store and, along with my own groceries, I buy a few things for Cora Mae from a list she gives me.

I'm now starting to see the complications of finding chauffeurs to drive me around to investigate crimes.

"Nah, it's only down the road." Cora Mae swung her purse and eyed my expanding midriff. "Exercise is good for you."

I found a flashlight in the closet, handed it to her, and watched her walk down the side of the road. Then I plunked down in front of the television to wait for Little Donny.

TWO

Word for the Day
SIMPATICO (sim PAHT i koh) adj.
Gets along well with or goes well
with another; compatible.

"Where were you last night?" I asked Little Donny the next morning when he staggered to the table.

I finished writing my new word on a scrap of paper and included the pronunciation since it wasn't an easy one to say—it sounded Italian.

Little Donny looked like he'd partied too hard and smelled like stale beer and probably would have stayed in bed if I hadn't rolled him out.

"Herb's Bar." Little Donny rubbed his red-rimmed eyes and squinted at me through narrow slits. "What time is it?"

"Way past time for you to drive me over to Chester's house. I have some investigating to do."

"What happened to your hair?" Little Donny's eyes were peeling open. His hand held his head, keeping it from flopping on the kitchen table. I set a bowl of cornflakes down so if his hand gave out he'd have something soft to fall into.

"I'll be waiting outside." I ruffled his hair as I passed.

George Erikson sat in a plastic lawn chair under the apple tree. I walked over to talk to him, since Little Donny was moving slow and I had a wait ahead of me before he could pull himself together and come out. Wasting time with George wasn't exactly a hardship.

George's father, Old Ben Erikson, and Barney developed a close friendship in spite of their age difference, and after Barney died, Old Ben told me he'd promised Barney he would look after me if anything ever happened to Barney. I thought he needed more taking care of than I did, but nothing could dissuade him. He'd made a promise and he'd keep his promise, but that's a Swede. Loyal to the last.

So Old Ben sent his son around every day to do odds and ends and when he died in the spring at the ripe old age of eighty-nine, his son kept coming round.

I have a small Christmas tree business that brings in enough money to pay the property taxes. George trims the trees twice a year, then cuts and wraps them for sale in late November during hunting season. This year, I plan on sharing the profits with him even though he's refused in the past.

George is a few years younger than I am, sixty, give or take a few years. He wears flannel shirts, colored t-shirts, and his trademark cowboy hat with a stuffed rattlesnake wrapped around the crown. You can see its fangs like it's about to strike.

Oh, and his buns are still tight. I may be getting old, but my eyes still work. He looks great in blue jeans. George used to be a construction foreman but quit to go into business for himself as a carpenter. He has that lean, mean, construction physique.

George and I are simpatico; we have the same view of life: take it easy, but don't forget to grab the gusto.

"What happened to your hair?" he said, amusement shining in his eyes.

"Celebrating hunting season." I stuffed the hunting cap back on my head and tucked the loose strands under it. I sat down on a chair next to him and could feel the cold of the plastic working into my legs and thighs.

"I hear Chester Lampi took a bullet yesterday," George said, adjusting his cowboy hat. He still had a full head of hair under the hat, dark brown with a touch of gray at the temples. "A stray bullet, they say."

"I don't know about that stray bullet business," I said. "It seems too convenient to me. What do you know about Chester?"

"Kept to himself." George had Barney's chain saw between his boots and began rubbing oil in the joints with a rust-colored rag. "He's got a son who lives east of town. The son got married last month—a blonde from down south someplace. Chester wasn't happy about it. Marrying an outsider and all."

Chester wouldn't have been happy about that.

We don't have Blacks, Mexicans, Puerto Ricans, or Asians in Stonely. Finns and Swedes settled the area. Culturally diverse to the people here means some fool sold his property to a Polack or a Kraut.

I'm more German than anything else, which I guess makes me one of those cultural diversities, and the word Kraut has been dropped one or two times within my hearing. My maiden name was Miller. I met Barney in Washington, D.C., in 1956 after arriving from my family farm in rural Ohio and finding work as a bookkeeper for the State Department. He was a marine stationed there and I fell in love with him the moment I laid eyes on him. I always loved a man in uniform.

I came home with him to Stonely. People weren't too happy about that, either. Times never change, and some haven't forgotten that I don't really belong. Forty-some years in the U.P. doesn't give you automatic citizenship. You need three or four generations for that.

"I ran into Chester at Ray's last week," George said, working the oil around the metal of the saw.

Ray owns the general store on Main Street and sells hardware, gun supplies, and gasoline, and he has a pretty good stock of grocery items. "Chester told me he was thinking about getting a winter home in Florida."

"Yeah, right," I said. When toads fly. Chester was dirt poor. His house wasn't much bigger than that hunting blind they hauled him out of. In fact, the hunting blind was built better. "He must have been kidding with you."

"No, he was serious."

"Sounds suspicious to me and worth checking out."

"Everything sounds suspicious to you. I suppose you think Chester was murdered." When I didn't answer, George looked up from greasing the chain saw and raised his eyebrows. Here we go again, his eyebrows said. I noticed he couldn't do that one eyebrow thing that Cora Mae's so good at.

"It sounds like Chester came into some money all of a sudden."

George shrugged.

"What was Chester buying at Ray's?"

George thought it over. "I don't know. It was already bagged."

George didn't know it, but he was sitting this very minute right on top of my buried treasure. After Barney's funeral and burial in the Trenary cemetery, Blaze drove me over to the Escanaba bank, and I hauled out every penny I own. Barney and I were savers our whole life so it amounted to quite a stockpile. I made Blaze wait outside so he wouldn't find out what I was doing and try to interfere.

The teller had to get the manager to approve the whole thing. He tried to talk me out of closing our account, but I stood firm. When I make up my mind, nobody can change it. I filled a grocery bag with the bills as the teller counted them out, then stuffed an old shirt on top to conceal the money.

Never trust the federal government, I say. They're out to get you. That crooked president, the IRS, all of them, a bunch of thieves waiting to pounce on good, law-abiding citizens the minute you turn your back.

Barney didn't see eye to eye with me on this issue, but once he was gone I went and rescued our money. I buried it in a steel box right under where George had his tight buns parked, right under the apple tree Barney and I planted the first year we were married. I know it's safe and I don't need it right now anyway. My Social Security is enough to live on, but it'll be waiting for me when Social

Security runs out of money one of these days, when that bunch of thieves in Washington steals it all.

The cold from the plastic lawn chair numbed my thighs and sent chills shooting down my legs. I stood up and shook them out. Flecks of snow swirled in the breeze and the ground was crunchy with frost. I wore wool socks with my boots and long underwear under my hunting jacket, but George sat casually in a white long-sleeved tee shirt and unbuttoned red flannel. His nipples stood out in the cold like bird dogs pointing.

"Time to put on a jacket, George."

"Not till January, Gertie. You know my rule. No coats till January."

I can live with that.

Bear Creek snakes around Tamarack Township, passing through the boundary line of my back forty. It also meanders through Chester's land. I left Little Donny in the truck and trudged through the low spot between the blind and the creek, looking for clues to Chester's death. I carried my twelve-gauge shotgun just in case. I wasn't sure what I was looking for, so I kept my eyes sharp.

Chester's blind was perfectly situated, a few yards off of Deer Run, a series of deer paths heavily traveled by herds of deer. City folks think deer leap every which way through the woods, but they don't. They have their own road system, and Deer Run is one of their superhighways.

This section of the path wound through some marshy low land with reeds and old cattails poking up, and ahead I could see young tamarack trees framing the ridge. My boots crunched through a thin layer of ice as I went. It was slow going because if I stepped in too deep, I would have water over the top of my boots. I tested each step and occasionally looked back at my sunken footsteps.

Eventually, I reached the ridge and continued following Deer Run down the other side to the creek. The creek water still flowed, with a thin crust of ice beginning to form on the surface. A young turkey, startled by my presence, rose in the air and, with enormous effort, cleared the top of the trees. I'm always fascinated watching those big birds fly.

When I could no longer feel my nose, I headed back, taking a smaller deer path. It veered west of my original trail and crossed over the ridge. Reaching the low marsh, I spotted broken ice patches leading toward Chester's blind. The same kind my boots made coming out, only I hadn't come through this way.

I followed the broken ice, trying to match my footsteps with the broken patches, but whoever came through had a wider stride than I did. About fifty yards out, the footsteps widened as though the owner began to hurry, perhaps running. I paused and looked around. From here I could see Chester's blind. With a high-powered scope, I could easily hit it. I considered giving it a try with my shotgun, but the weight of it was making my arm feel like it was wrapped in concrete, and I would have a hard time explaining to Blaze why buckshot was plastered in the side of the blind. I already would have some explaining to do if Blaze found out I tromped all over potential evidence, but it couldn't be helped. Someone had to investigate.

Looking down, I saw something shiny lying under a thin patch of ice. I broke through with my boot and picked it up. It was a spent rifle shell. My heart started to pound in my ears. When the pounding subsided, I rummaged in my jacket, found a tissue, gently wrapped the shell, and tucked it into my pocket.

Little Donny was sound asleep in the truck, his head thrown back on the headrest, his mouth wide open. I took the opportunity to snitch the girly magazines out of Chester's blind to show to Cora Mae. There were some hot male bodies in there, too.

———

"What the hell were you doing back there in the first place?" Blaze yelled. "And you, why were you helping her?" Now he was glaring at Little Donny and jabbing his index finger at Little Donny's chest. "Keep your hands off my pa's truck, Little Donny, if you can't keep her out of my business. Next time I see you behind the wheel of that truck and her sitting next to you, I'm pulling you over and arresting you for obstructing justice. Do you understand?"

"Okay, okay, I get it."

"And the next time. . . ."

"You can't do that," I interrupted. "That's my truck and you can't arrest him for driving it." I turned to Little Donny and patted his knee. "Don't worry. He can't do that."

"I'm the sheriff. I can do anything I want to."

"But you didn't let me finish. Look at what I have." I pulled the tissue out of my pocket and carefully unwrapped the shell. "Evidence."

Blaze wasn't looking at the shell. He seemed to notice me for the first time. "What the hell happened to your hair?"

He sat at my kitchen table sucking down all my sugar doughnuts. His eyesore yellow truck was still running in the driveway and a cloud of smoke-like exhaust hovered over the truck, a sure sign that it was cold outside.

I ignored that last question and explained where I found the shell and about the footprints in the ice. Blaze didn't look happy but it didn't stop him from continuing to stuff his face.

"And I want you to test it for fingerprints," I finished, pleased with myself. I thought about having DETECTIVE JOHNSON printed on the side of my truck.

"You've been interfering with my work again." Blaze wiped his hands on a napkin. "Did you ever think that maybe I was going to check back there using proper police procedures? Did you ever think to check with me first?"

"No, I didn't. Knowing you, you already closed the case, calling it an accident." That was Blaze's style and we both knew it.

"Did you ever think that maybe you screwed up a crime scene? Anywhere else you'd try a stunt like that, you'd be arrested for interfering with a police investigation."

"Then you're admitting it was a crime."

Blaze's nostrils spread out and his face turned the color of an overripe tomato.

"Floyd Tatrow came by for a lie detector test last night. I suppose you don't know anything about that?"

"Not a thing," I said.

"What have I done to deserve you?" Blaze shouted, throwing his arms up in the air. I could tell he was getting ready to go into all my past sins against him. He was the most paranoid person I ever met. "Why do I put up with this?" he continued, rising from the table. "You know what you are? You're the family curse."

I settled in for a go-around, which, I could have reminded Blaze, I always win. I stood up next to him and leaned in close.

"You put up with it for a lot of reasons, Doughnut Boy. You put up with it for those freebies you're stuffing in your mouth, for one. You put up with it for the free rent, for another."

This was one of those times I was talking about earlier when I don't appreciate the close family ties quite as much as I could.

Blaze reached for the rifle shell and gave me an angry scowl.

"Be careful with that," I said. "I don't want your fingerprints fouling up the works. And I need the name and address for Chester's son."

There was a long silence, then, "Why?"

"I'm going to interrogate him. See what I can turn up."

"I'll arrest you if you do."

There was a loud bang as Blaze slammed out the door.

———

"Blaze is still mad about the horse thing," Star said over the telephone when I called her. "He sure does hold a grudge a long time."

My baby, Star, and I used to talk on the phone every day, but lately she hasn't been around much. She swore off men after her good-for-nothing husband finally ran off, but it looks like she's getting back in the saddle. She's being coy about it, though.

"He says he changed his name to Brian," I told her. I was washing dishes, trying not to clang pans while I talked. I had the phone on my right shoulder, wedged between my head and shoulder.

"Ma, nobody takes him seriously. Sometimes they call him Bucky or Bronco to tease him. But he's tried to change it to Brian for years. Where have you been?"

"I've been busy."

My other kids never complained about the names I chose for them. Star and Heather were happy, so I couldn't figure Blaze out. Blaze is a nice name—original, manly. "He has a John Wayne name," I said.

"He has John Wayne's horse's name," Star said.

At least I should get points for originality. I didn't name them Barney Junior, Barney Senior, and Barney the Third.

"Do you know the name of Chester's son?" I asked Star, steering the conversation in the right direction. "I heard he lives on the east side of Stonely toward Trenary."

"Wasn't it terrible what happened to Chester? I think his son's name is Bill. Bill Lampi."

"Thanks, sweetie. I just wish Blaze and I were more simpatico." I pronounced it slowly, reading from my scrap of paper.

"What?"

"It's my word for the day," I explained. "Blaze must be under a lot of stress. He threatened to arrest me today."

"I'm sure he didn't mean it. Just don't give him a reason."

———

Cora Mae almost fell off her high-heel boots when she came out and saw me driving Barney's truck up her driveway. "Whee! You can drive!"

I didn't tell her that I rammed a big hole the size of a meteor in the side of the barn when I accidentally shifted into forward instead of reverse. I was starting to get the hang of it, except for braking. I silently thanked Cora Mae for her circle driveway. I wouldn't have to try to back down.

"Hop in."

Cora wore a black turtleneck sweater, black stretch pants, and a fake fur vest jacket, also black.

"I told you to wear orange, Cora Mae. Out-of-town hunters are creeping all over the place. You look like a black bear. One of them is going to shoot your buns off."

"Honey, orange just isn't my color, but I can see it's yours."

Another hair joke. And from the woman who did it to me.

I was working on a quick comeback when I accidentally slammed on the brakes at the bottom of Cora Mae's driveway instead of the gas.

Cora flew forward.

"Better put on your seatbelt till I get the hang of this," I said, starting up again.

Chester lived in a cracker box about a quarter mile from his hunting blind. You could see he wasn't much of a handyman because the house was an eyesore—peeling green paint, rotting wood porch, bare windows.

Cora stepped gingerly over a gaping hole in the porch and peeked into the front window. "No one's home, Gertie. We better come back another time."

"Of course no one's home. Chester's wife's been in her grave for years, and since Chester's dead, we can safely assume he isn't going to answer the door."

"But why are we standing here if you knew no one was going to let us in?" Cora Mae's penciled eyebrows were shaped like a question mark and she looked at me like I had ruined her day. I would have thought the ride over with me driving for the first time would have been excitement enough.

I grinned and held up a screwdriver and a hammer from Barney's toolbox. "We have work to do on the back door. Come on."

I planned on prying between the doorjamb and the lock with a screwdriver, but peeking in, I noticed the lock was a deadbolt. It's impossible to pry a deadbolt. I found that out last time I locked myself out of my house after losing my keys.

I tried turning the knob to see if the door was unlocked, which probably should have been my first step, but it didn't matter since the door really was locked.

I tried tapping gently on the glass with my hammer. Then I hauled off and smacked the window a sharp blow. Glass shattered at our feet. I said, "Oops," as Cora Mae and I looked down simultaneously. I knocked the rest of the glass out of the doorframe with the hammer, stuck my hand through, and unlocked the door.

We began searching in the kitchen. The place was a mess. Piles of litter overflowing from the garbage can, six weeks of dirty dishes stacked on the counter and scattered throughout the house, clothes tossed over chairs.

I made notes in a spiral notebook in case something might be important later. My eye for detail is dead on, but my memory gets fuzzy now and then. I was careful to include everything, since clues to solving the case could be anywhere.

In the living room, I noticed three guns resting in the gun rack next to the television and an old sofa with a dirty blanket draped over it shoved against a gray wall. I also noticed things that weren't there. There weren't any drapes or shades on the windows, and there weren't any more smut magazines.

We pulled out every drawer and went through every closet without finding anything unusual. I took a broom from the kitchen and swept up the glass and removed the shards still embedded in the frame of the window. I dumped the whole mess in a cardboard box and decided to haul it home with me to dispose of it.

"If all the window glass is gone," I reasoned out loud to Cora Mae, "it might take longer for it to be discovered. Nothing like a pile of glass on the floor to draw attention where you don't want it drawn." I reached through the window and relocked the door.

I hit Chester's mailbox with the bumper of Barney's pickup truck on the way out and bent the post a bit, but likely he wouldn't mind even if he were still alive.

After dropping Cora Mae at her house, I headed home. The hole in the barn wall was a gaping reminder of my driving skills, and now guinea hens ran around the yard, squawking angrily.

Guinea hens are useful for ridding your yard of wood ticks and deer ticks, which is quite a mission considering the diseases ticks carry. Guinea hens cluster together and move around the yard looking for bugs to eat and making a lot of noises. Since I brought home these twelve guineas, I haven't had a single tick slip through.

They're a lot of work in the winter months, though. The raccoons like to snack on them, so I have to be careful to keep them inside at night and I have to buy feed for them.

I looked at the sky, which was darkening rapidly, and studied the guinea hen situation. I crossed the drive and looked for Little Donny in the house, but he wasn't there.

Hauling the hens two by two, one under each arm, into the house, I shut them in the bathroom. It took a while because they started running from me after I caught the first two, probably thinking they were going to be tomorrow's dinner.

Worn out from the chasing, I collapsed on the couch, my heart racing.

I was going to take a short break and then call George to repair the barn enough to hold the hens, but I must have drifted off for a spell. The next thing I knew, Little Donny was screaming and birds were running through the house flapping their wings, trying to go airborne.

I sprang up and surveyed the situation.

Little Donny, leaning against the wall next to the bathroom, held both hands clutched over his heart like he'd had the scare of his life. A hen screeched at his feet. Another one sprung across the couch. This was a full-scale invasion.

I walked over to Little Donny and pulled the startled kid in for a big hug while the hens ran everywhere. Little Donny's shoulders started shaking and I hoped he wasn't crying. A scare can do that to you. He had tears running down his face all right, but he was laughing. I chimed in until my sides started aching.

Little Donny managed to herd the hens back in the bathroom while I called George. He brought a large pen in the back of his truck and we transferred the guinea hens from the bathroom to the pen.

George took a good look at the hole in the barn, glanced at my new red hair, then studied the hole again.

"Did a meteorite shoot through here?" he wanted to know. "Didn't hear we were expecting a meteor shower. Must have been a huge one."

He glanced back at the truck, which was parked next to the hole.

"Don't know how it happened," I lied.

George grinned.

THREE

Word for the Day
MACHINATIONS (MAK uh NA shuns) n.
An artful or secret plot or scheme, especially
one with evil intent.

IN THE U.P. WE take deer hunting seriously. For most of us it isn't
sport, it's survival. Of course, we make it fun. There's the hunter's
ball at the beginning of the season, a banquet down at the senior
citizen's center on the last day of hunting season, and a few other
events thrown in between. But we can't afford to fill our freezers
with sides of beef and slabs of pork, so instead we hunt and fish
like our ancestors, and we count on dressing out at least two deer
every season to see us through.

Little Donny still didn't have his first one, and it was day three
of hunting season. If things didn't improve soon, I wouldn't have

venison through the winter. Even if he managed to get in a shot, I didn't have a lot of confidence in his shooting ability after watching him target practice last year.

Target practicing is Tamarack County's favorite hobby when we aren't hunting. I've never been a hunter—can't stand seeing an animal dying right before my eyes—but I love target practice. Little Donny's shooting problem exists because he doesn't show up until hunting season begins, and since target practicing during hunting season will make your neighbors want to hang *you* in the garage instead of a deer, we can't work on getting him in shooting shape. I bet Little Donny hasn't fired his rifle since last summer.

A slew of black flies had hatched out and swarmed around my living room picture window. I pulled the Hoover out of the closet and was sucking the flies up in the vacuum when Little Donny came out of his bedroom dressed for hunting.

"You're never going to have any luck if you don't get out to the blind earlier than this," I said, glancing at the kitchen clock. It was eight-thirty.

He eyed the vacuum cleaner. "What are you doing?"

"Cleaning house. Haven't you ever seen anyone clean house before?" I bent to my task, working the hose around the edges of the window.

Little Donny watched for a while like he'd never seen anyone vacuum flies before. How else did he think I'd get them out of the house? Open the door and ask them to leave?

He grabbed a cinnamon roll from the counter and his rifle from the rack and headed out in the direction of the hunting shack.

Ten minutes later a process server from Escanaba banged on my door, insisted I sign a paper, and handed me an envelope. "Consider yourself served," he said.

———

After struggling through the legal jargon twice and still not fully understanding what I was reading, I picked up the phone and called Little Donny's father, Big Donny. If anyone could understand fancy legal talk, it was Heather's city husband.

"You're required to appear in probate court," he explained after listening to me read the papers. "For a guardianship hearing."

"Whose guardianship?"

There was a pause. "Yours."

"Why would I need a guardian?"

"Blaze is petitioning the court to become your guardian. He obviously feels you need someone to take care of your personal finances. Has he talked to you about this?"

"We've been arguing nonstop ever since Barney died. He wants me to hand over my money so he can take care of it. He's lost his mind."

"It's not an issue of placement, which is good," Big Donny said. "That means he's not trying to force you into a nursing home."

"Might as well be."

"If you decide to contest it he has to prove you're incompetent to manage your own affairs."

"It says here that I pose a substantial risk of harm to myself and to others." I couldn't believe my own son would do this to me. When have I ever harmed myself or anybody else?

"Better get yourself an attorney," Big Donny advised.

———

I was sitting at the kitchen table, feeling sorry for myself, when the police scanner jumped to life.

I grabbed my shotgun and truck keys and ran for the door.

Blaze's sheriff's truck was parked in Chester's driveway and he stood on the broken porch talking to Betty Berg, who lived across the road from Chester. She used to be a friend to my Star, until Betty played find-the-weenie with Star's now ex-husband. She isn't on our Christmas list, that's for sure.

Blaze watched me drive in, his hands on his hips, his mouth hanging wide open in disbelief.

I parked as far from his truck as possible to give myself plenty of maneuvering room when I wanted to leave, then jumped out of the truck. I decided to wait for some privacy to confront Blaze on the guardianship hearing issue. Besides, murder was more serious.

"What's happened here?" I called out. "Who called the report in? Was that you, Betty?" Figures it would be Betty. Betty's nose was longer than Cora Mae's string of men.

"That's right, Gertie. That was me. I came over to peek in the window, just to make sure everything was all right, and imagine my surprise. Come and take a look-see."

Star should have let her lousy husband have Betty instead of putting up a fight. It would have taught him a valuable lesson.

Betty was cute a few years ago, but she'd really let herself go bad. She wore a fuzzy housecoat with yellow and pink flowers and weighed in at a good two-eighty, a real tub of lard. She held her arms around herself like she was cold, although dressed up in all that fat, it didn't seem likely.

"Hold everything," Blaze shouted while Betty and I peeked through the front window. I turned and saw he wasn't on the porch anymore. He stood by my truck, pointing at it with one arm and waving me over with the other. Like he was directing traffic. "Come back here, Ma."

I hoped with the excitement of the break-in and all, Blaze would be distracted from the fact that I was driving, but I wasn't that lucky. I stepped off the rotting porch.

"Anything new?" he asked when he saw he had my attention. "You know, anything at all?"

"Let's save the family chitchat for later. We have a break-in to investigate at the moment."

"We're going to talk about this right now." Blaze, forgetting to lower his arm, was still pointing at the truck with his index finger. "When did you start driving?"

"A while ago. Cora Mae taught me."

"And do you have a license?"

"What kind of license do you want? A hunting license, or a private investigator license? No, I don't have a private investigator license. Yet." The key to winning a round with Blaze is to frazzle him. Once he loses his temper, he can't think straight and it's an automatic win for my side.

"No, Ma, I mean a DRIVING LICENSE."

"You don't need to shout. I'm not deaf, you know. Of course I have a driver's license," I lied. "I went to Escanaba and got one right after you threatened poor Little Donny."

Before Blaze could regroup, I turned quickly and caught up with Betty, who was still peering through the window. I looked in.

Yesterday the condition of the house reminded me of a football scrimmage gone awry; it was a war zone today. The garbage can had been dumped out on the floor, for starters. Cabinets were pulled open and the contents thrown every which way.

Blaze scurried up behind us. "We'll finish this conversation after I check out the house."

I made a mental note to vanish before he finished his "investigation."

"Wonder how they gained entry," our local sheriff said, and began walking around the house. "Well, look at this." He stopped at the back entrance, eyeing up the door. "Smashed the glass to get in."

I wasn't going to be the one to point out the missing glass. Betty took care of that.

"But there isn't any broken glass on the floor," Miss Betty Snoop Berg said. "Isn't that odd?"

Blaze didn't respond. He tried the door then reached through and unlocked it.

"Wait out here," he said, closing the door behind him.

I waited until he rounded the corner and disappeared into the bedroom, then I followed. "You wait here," I said to Betty over my shoulder. "Like Blaze said. We don't want any accidental tampering with evidence."

There wasn't a drawer or closet or cupboard that hadn't been stripped. Everything was piled on the floor—clothes, dishes, and papers. Nothing obvious seemed to be missing as far as I could tell, not that Chester had much to steal, but the television was still here and so were the guns in the gun rack.

Blaze and I ran into each other in the bedroom doorway and we both shrieked.

"I told you to wait outside, Ma."

I decided since Blaze was busy trying to ruin my life, he was through telling me what to do. "If this was a robbery, wouldn't the guns be the first thing they'd take?" I said. "Proves this wasn't a robbery. Someone was looking for something."

Blaze scribbled in his little book, and when he closed it up I could tell he was closing the case. "Kids probably, vandalizing, heard about Chester and knew the place was empty. There's a group of real troublemakers over on the other side of Trenary. I'll check it out." He walked over to his truck, reached in for his radio, and made a call.

Standing on the porch with Two-Ton Mama, hoping she wasn't about to punch another hole in the porch, I realized that I must have played some role in the stunted development of my one and only son, but for the life of me I couldn't sort it out.

I was hauling myself up into the truck to make my escape before Blaze finished on the radio when a thought struck me. I pulled my notebook out of the glove compartment and flipped it open to the entries from my search of Chester's house. I jumped back out and ran to the window for another look. I was right.

Blaze walked over.

"Come look at this." Outwardly, I tried to appear cool and collected, but inside I was dancing the jig. "Something's rotten in Finland. There were three weapons in Chester's gun rack yesterday, and now there are four. Four. Where did that extra one come from?"

"I know I don't really expect an honest answer," Blaze said, "but I'll ask anyway. How do you know how many guns were in there yesterday?"

"I stopped by to pay my respects?"

"And who did you visit with? The ghost of Chester's past?"

"Well, maybe I stopped by just to look around. Remember I'm part of this investigation."

"You're not part of this investigation. And you're going to stop interfering. Seems like we had a conversation just yesterday about you and interfering. What did you do, run right over here?" Blaze stared at me. "Wait. It's become clear. . . ."

He hitched up his belt and glanced at Betty. "You can go now. We're pretty much finished."

Betty wasn't about to move from her front row seat at the boxing match, so Blaze hooked his arm through mine and walked me off the porch.

His voice was low in my ear. "Yes, it's all clear now, like looking through broken glass. You broke in the back door, didn't you? You came over here, probably with the Black Widow, and you illegally broke in. That's why there isn't any glass on the floor. You swept it up."

"I only wanted to look for evidence. The window was an accident. And the house wasn't torn apart like it is now."

Blaze released my arm, leaned against his truck, and buried his face in both his hands.

"I've got to go," I said and hightailed it to the truck before Blaze remembered to ask for my driver's license.

"Tell Star I say hi," Betty called out, waving a chunky arm over her head.

Right. Sure thing. The nerve of some people.

———

On the way over to George's, I made a mental list of the information I had so far. A dead body, footprints cracking through ice, a rifle shell, sudden and unexplained money—if Chester really meant the comment about a place in Florida—and finally, too many guns on the gun rack. It was plain as the nose on Blaze's face that someone had murdered Chester, and it was obvious that I would have to be the one to catch the murderer.

After a year of mourning, I was ready for action, ready to make a contribution to my community. I was on a mission.

Distracted from my driving, I missed the turn into George's driveway and ended up with the two right tires hanging over into a culvert. I threw the gears into reverse and revved the engine, trying to rock the truck back and forth the same way I'd seen Barney rock it when he was stuck in snow, but nothing worked.

Leaving the truck in the ditch, I walked the half-mile up to George's house in my heavy hunting boots. I was winded by the time I got there, and feeling every one of my sixty-six years.

George was a jack-of-all-trades, and his yard looked like the town dump, littered with car frames and parts, a variety of tractors, and piles of old lumber. Running around in the mess were all kinds of animals. Mules, goats, chickens—you name it, at one time George had it. He also was the unofficial county dogcatcher. Several dogs in wire kennels began howling and barking when they caught sight of me.

I found George in one of his three outbuildings, welding a metal frame. He had on an undershirt, the sleeveless kind. The temperature, I guessed, must be about twenty-five degrees, warming to a balmy thirty or so where he worked. And he's not even wearing a shirt. What a man!

He acknowledged me with a nod and went back to concentrating on his work. I sat on the edge of a large workbench and watched George's rippling biceps, then started playing with the equipment lying on the table. I picked up something that looked like a miniature cattle prod and tried to figure out how to turn it on.

"Stay away from that, Gertie." George pulled off a pair of safety glasses and walked over.

"What is it?"

"A stun gun. I don't use it much, but it comes in handy if I have a stubborn animal, like that mule out there, that won't go where I need it to go. Or if I pick up a stray dog and it attacks me. But I never use it unless I absolutely have to."

"How does it stay juiced?" I said, intrigued with the device. It would fit in my purse perfectly.

"Battery pack. There's an extra one around here someplace." George opened a cardboard box and sorted through a tangle of electrical cords. "Here it is."

"I need to borrow it for a little while."

"Don't know why you'd have any use for a stun gun."

"There's been a stray dog hanging around by the shed, looks scrawny and wild to me. Maybe if I zap him he'll decide to move on." I was getting good at lying, but I figure it comes with the job, a curse of the detective business. I couldn't very well tell George I was on the trail of a savage killer and I needed protection. My shotgun is handy, but I can't haul it everywhere, and it's no good at close range.

"Haven't noticed any wild dogs over by you."

"He's there," I insisted. "Mean, ugly, and he has yellow eyes. Has wolf or coyote in him, I bet."

George handed me the stun gun. "Better have Little Donny shoot him if he gets the chance. He might be rabid."

I stuffed the stun gun into my purse and I was right—it was a perfect fit. Then I remembered why I stopped by in the first place.

"I'm having family over for supper tonight. Thought you might like to come. I'm making venison steaks."

"Can't. But thank you kindly." George grinned. "Sure do hate to miss one of your family get-togethers."

I was disappointed since I like to have George at our family meals to run interference for me with Grandma Johnson, who spends all her spare time dreaming up nasty comments to try out on me.

"Will you have time to fix the hole in my barn before they come over?" I asked.

George laughed and shook his head. "No. I'll stop by and take another look at it, but it's going to take a couple of days."

"I have one more little favor to ask." I began to explain why I left the truck at the end of the drive. What I like most about

46

George is that he isn't judgmental. He accepts everyone for what they are and doesn't make me feel foolish.

He helped me pull the truck out of the ditch, then followed me home to look at the repair job.

———

We were standing in the driveway when Little Donny pulled up next to us driving a blue Ford station wagon. I recognized it. Carl Anderson bought it two weeks ago and had been showing it off to everyone.

Little Donny rolled the window down, and you could tell he thought he had bagged Big Buck, our legendary eighteen-pointer. "Look what I shot over at Carl's place."

George walked around and looked in the window. I followed. In the back of the wagon, on a wad of black plastic garbage bags, lay a little spike-horned deer.

"A little guy," George said.

"What? He's a good size, isn't he, Granny?"

"I can still see the spots on him," I said to Little Donny.

Little Donny turned around in the driver's seat to take a look, and at that exact moment the little spike lifted its head and stared back at astonished Little Donny. You could see that Little Donny would like to have opened the door and beat it out of there, but with George and me looking on, he had to make a stand.

The deer and Little Donny leapt into action together. The deer started pounding on the windows with his hooves. Little Donny flew out of the front seat, opened the back door, and dove in. He grabbed the little buck by the horns and held on.

"Go git him," George said, and closed the car door behind Donny. I wasn't sure which one of them George was talking to, and I couldn't imagine what Little Donny was trying to do.

The deer's horns were making an awful mess of Carl's brand new station wagon.

"You call it," George said to me as we stood, watching.

"The little spike. My money's on the little spike."

"Sure win," George said, then to Little Donny, "Watch the horns, they're wicked."

When Little Donny's nose started gushing blood, I decided it was time for action. I couldn't send him home to Heather gored by a deer. I dug the stun gun out of my purse, jerked the car door open, aimed at the spike, and zapped.

I could smell that new car smell and something else. I sniffed. Something like burnt wires.

Little Donny let go of the horns. His head hit the car window with a thud like a bird flying into a window. He started twitching.

George opened the back hatch and the deer uncurled itself from the wagon and zigzagged with flying leaps out to the woods.

We helped Little Donny into the house when he could finally stand up. His hair sprung from his head like he'd been hit by a bolt of lightning, and he couldn't talk without slobbering.

The good thing is, now I know it really works.

"Next time you shoot at a deer," I advised him, "make sure it's dead before you load it in your car."

———

Little Donny sat on the couch, his hair every which way, when the family began arriving. He still couldn't talk, and his eyes were unfocused. George had said a hasty goodbye after making sure Little Donny didn't need medical attention.

Star drove over on her ex-husband's ATV, wearing a fake fur jacket she had dyed orange for hunting season, a pair of mukluks, and a sassy orange and blue feather hat. Star, my baby, had turned forty-one in September, which she took hard at the time. She obviously is bouncing back. Petite, like me, she looked real spiffy in her new jacket.

She carried in a bowl of creamed rutabaga, set it on the table, and hung her jacket on the coat rack by the front door. By then, I saw Blaze and Mary drive in.

I wouldn't say it out loud, but Mary's the mousiest, plainest-minded woman I've ever met. You could meet her ten times in a week and never remember her from one time to the next. She named her daughters after her—Mary Jane and Mary Elizabeth—and they're both just as drab.

"Can I help?" Mary asked after she hung up her coat.

"I'll let you know in a little while if I need help. Right now you just have a seat in the living room and make yourself comfortable while I pound these steaks."

I picked up a hammer and began thumping the meat. Most people, unless they're old timers or are trained by the old timers, don't know how to cook good venison. A steak, in particular, is tricky. First you have to pound it with a hammer on both sides until it has holes clear through it like Swiss cheese. Then salt and pepper it all over, and quick fry it in butter. The butter's important. If you use oil you'll ruin it. Afterwards the cook gets to sop up the pan drippings with a piece of bread.

I consider myself a pretty good cook.

"What's wrong with Little Donny?" Star called to me.

"Nothing's wrong with Little Donny," I said.

"His eyes are twitching and he won't say anything."

"He's tired. He had a hard day hunting and all." Maybe I should have laid Little Donny out on the couch, closed his eyes, and said he was sleeping. Leaving him propped up was a mistake. "I'm going to start frying the steaks. Tell Blaze to mosey over and pick up Grandma Johnson."

As we were putting the food on the table, Blaze arrived with his grandmother in tow. We grabbed our seats and dug right in.

"Why don't anybody ever pick me up till the food's on the table?" Grandma Johnson wanted to know. "I like to visit too, and I know all a you was here ahead a time."

We concentrated hard on our meal, pretending like we hadn't heard.

"And what did you go and do to your hair? Every time I see you, you've done something foolish to yourself."

My mother-in-law is ninety-two and doesn't appear to be running down. She still keeps her own house, with everyone taking turns stopping in and helping out. If you ask her the secret to living a long life she'll tell you it's what you eat—lots of vegetables and suck candy. You know, she'll say, that hard stuff like anise and butterscotch.

But I think she stays young taking potshots at me.

"Come and eat," I called to Little Donny. "Won't be anything left if you don't hurry up."

"Noth righth now," Little Donny said.

"I'll make you a plate for later."

"Place is going to pot," Grandma Johnson said, swinging her head around like that possessed girl in the *Exorcist*. "I bet Barney is turning in his grave over the looks of this place. Did you see the hole in the side of the barn, Blaze?"

Blaze doesn't like to be interrupted while he's eating, but Grandma Johnson's hard to ignore when she's right in your face. His mouth was stuffed with red potatoes.

I briefly thought about confronting Blaze about the court papers right at the dinner table, right in front of the entire family. But I wasn't sure they'd side with me, especially Grandma Johnson.

"First thing tomorrow I want you to fix that hole for your ma," she continued.

"Yes, Grandma," Blaze said through his mouthful, glancing at me. I gave him a cold smile.

"I hear you're helping on one of the cases," Mary said to me.

"Not anymore," Blaze said.

"This apple pie is pretty good, considerin' how bad your baking usually is," Grandma Johnson said. "I used to feel so sorry for Barney, havin' to eat what you baked."

A piece of apple pie with whipped cream topping called to me from the table. I wanted to smear it in Grandma Johnson's face. Picking up the plate, the urge became stronger and stronger, but Mary must have read my mind because she softly called my name. When I looked over, our eyes met, and she shook her head. Okay. When Grandma Johnson leaves maybe I'll zap her with the stun gun instead. I set the plate down.

"I love the pie," Mary said. "The crust is just right." She took another bite and hummed. Humming during a meal is a family tradition. If a meal is just right, the whole family takes turns humming. Except of course Grandma Johnson, who never hummed a note in her whole life. "Blaze said he had the rifle shell you found out at Chester's hunting shack tested. Isn't that right, Honey?"

Blaze leaned back in his chair and glared at his wife. Apparently he didn't want me to know how the case was progressing.

"Well?" I asked.

"Well nothing. There weren't any prints on the shell."

"The next step is to figure out what gun it was fired from." Though I was disappointed, I was still trying to be helpful in case Blaze didn't know the next step.

"Already did that. It was fired from Chester's own rifle, Ma. Nothing suspicious about it at all. Chester was probably target practicing before hunting season. That shell could have been laying there for awhile."

"How do you explain away the footprints coming from the creek, Einstein?"

"Chester's."

"What rifle was it fired from?" I asked.

"Top one in the gun rack."

"Didn't I tell you someone put a weapon in there after Chester died?"

"I only had the shell tested to prove you wrong," my son said. "And you're wrong. Nobody put a rifle back. You're wrong."

"Building evidence against me?"

"I don't need to, you built it against yourself."

Blaze and I were having a stare-down. We used to have stare-downs when he was a kid, but those were for fun. This was different. Blaze's stare was telling me I was old and feeble-minded and a pain in the backside. My stare was saying he sure wasn't Clint Eastwood or Mel Gibson. More like Don Knotts in Mayberry RFD. And a lousy son to boot.

He looked away first.

It was snowing hard outside by the time the table was cleared and the dishes washed and put away. Star roared away on her ATV, and Grandma Johnson headed for the bathroom. Little Donny slept like a baby on the couch, and Blaze sat in a chair, a pained expression on his face like he'd eaten one piece of pie too much.

"One of these days," I said to Mary after Grandma closed the bathroom door, "I'm going to tell her off."

"You think I'm deaf," Grandma Johnson called. "I can hear a cooked noodle hit the floor from across the house, and I heard that."

Mary and I laughed, and I took a good look at her. She was plain, all right—nobody would ever call her pretty—but she had a rosy face, like she was happy all the time. She and Blaze were having some trouble with one of their daughters. I keep telling them she's just young.

I remember being young, and it's a tough business. I wouldn't go back there for all the Christmas trees in Tamarack County, although I wouldn't mind shaving off a year or two. But being sixty-six has its advantages. You don't let anyone tell you what's what any more, and you don't have to pay so much attention to laws and rules. Break one and everyone just chalks it up to hardening of the brain. I like that.

At least I did until Blaze decided I really did have hardening of the brain.

Before drifting off to sleep, I realized I'd forgotten to use my word for the day. I guess I was thrown off by Blaze's disloyalty to his own mother.

I have more on my mind these days than I used to.

FOUR

Word for te Day
PICAYUNE (PIK uh YOON) adj.
Trivial or petty; small or small-minded.

Friday dawned cold and crisp, with a fresh blanket of snow on the ground. Little Donny was as good as new. He ate half a pound of bacon and three fried eggs, and was on his second cup of coffee when he remembered Carl's station wagon. He scrambled up and ran outside, forgetting his coat. He stood there a while staring at the car, then came in, stomping his boots on the rug, and collapsed at the kitchen table cradling his head in his hands.

"What am I going to tell Carl?"

"I called him last night and told him you'd bring his station wagon back today," I said. "You can clean it up some."

"The whole thing's a blur." Little Donny had a knot on his forehead the size of a baseball where he'd hit his head on the car window.

"That big old buck kicked you in the head," I lied. "That's why you can't remember much. What do you remember? Anything at all?"

Little Donny didn't answer. He groaned and went back to rocking his head. If Little Donny didn't remember getting zapped, I was home free. George would never tell.

"It happens sometimes. Nothing to be ashamed of. You fire at a deer," I explained, "and you don't know it, but the bullet just sort of grazes him, and then he plays possum or he's just stunned. Could have happened to anyone."

I instantly regretted saying stunned. It might trigger Little Donny's memory.

Little Donny looked at me through his fingers, then went back to rocking.

"Your Grandpa Barney lost one that way," I continued. "A nice eight-pointer he shot out at the blind. He went to get the tractor to pull it out of the woods, and when he got back it was gone. Just up and ran off."

Little Donny wasn't taking in anything I said.

I felt tired and stiff from cooking and entertaining company and tromping around on the investigation trail, and decided to head to my deer blind behind the house.

I use the blind as a retreat rather than for hunting. When the kids were little, I'd pull my gun from the rack and trudge out there while Barney babysat. No one ever thought to ask me why I never shot anything, but I think Barney knew. Old habits die hard, and so I still spend time there whenever I feel a need to get away from the rest of the world.

I needed to wind down and do some thinking about Chester's murder and my approaching court date.

George was working on the hole in the barn. His rattlesnake cowboy hat was all I could see as I shuffled by.

"Hey, George."

He raised his head and tipped his hat.

"I'm going to take a shot at Big Buck," I said, lifting my gun, and George nodded.

The air smelled like burning wood, my favorite smell. It was nippy out and I could see my breath fogging around my face. I wore long underwear under my hunting clothes, and I turned down the earflaps on my hat when I felt my ears begin to sting. I could hear my feet swishing through the fresh snow as I approached the shack. Apples and corn that I had thrown in a pile had been whittled down to next to nothing, and deer tracks crisscrossed everywhere.

I leaned the gun in the corner of the shack and started the propane heater, then settled into the worn La-Z-Boy to watch. I could hear wind whistling against the shack and the propane heater popping into high gear. Within minutes it was toasty warm inside the shack.

When I woke up, the last of the apples and corn had been eaten and half the day was gone. I stood and shook out my stiff joints, and admitted to myself that I wasn't a spring chicken anymore.

I replenished the apples and corn from a well-stocked barrel in the corner, closed up, and trudged back to get ready for Chester's funeral.

At three o'clock, I picked up Cora Mae and headed for Lacken's Funeral Home on the outskirts of town.

"I told Kitty we'd pick her up," Cora Mae said.

"No problem," I said, wondering how we were going to stuff her into the cab.

Kitty still sets her hair in pin curls, which went out of style a hundred years ago, and for good reason. Her short gray hair sticks out under bobby pins every which way like it's spring-loaded. She always has her head wired up to come visiting and I couldn't help wondering who was going to get to see the final product if not Cora Mae and me. Thinking back, I remember only a handful of times seeing Kitty without pin curls—weddings and funerals, mostly.

Since this was a funeral, we were in for a treat. Kitty waddled out without her bobby pins. She had combed through the front of her hair, but when she turned around to close her door, I noticed she had forgotten to brush out the back.

Kitty's overweight, always has been, and gravity's winning. Blubber hangs from her upper arms, and the front of her knees are dimpled. She wears housedresses and never learned to keep her legs together, so you can see her garter straps where they connect to her stockings. Most people look away. It's not a pretty sight.

We were all dressed in burial black. I hoped for two things tonight. One, to find the opportunity to talk to Chester's son, Bill, and two, to see how Ed Lacken hid the hole in Chester's forehead. Because Ed Lacken did the burying for everyone in the county, I hoped his work was still high quality. I wanted to be done up right when the time came. I know he did right by Barney.

Cora Mae was hoping for something entirely different.

"I heard that Onni Maki is some stud muffin since he's taking Viagra," my friend said. She sat between Kitty and me and had her knees and arms crushed tight against her body. Kitty was a tight fit in any truck.

"Onni Maki's an old has-been," I said, watching the road carefully in case I missed something in my first drive after dark. "Who'd want to see him naked?" I shuddered at the thought. We were all getting old and falling apart, but Onni Maki was falling apart faster than most of us.

"He looks like a plucked turkey," Kitty added, and I laughed.

"That's not true, and I aim to get some of the action," Cora Mae insisted. "Doesn't come around these parts often."

"There used to be a lot of rumors floating around about him when he was younger," Kitty said, shifting her weight. "Onni's always been a wild one. Fist fighting, drinking heavy, women." Kitty frowned in concentration. "I'll remember it all eventually."

I shook my head. "Kitty, you know everything about everybody. Where do you get your information?"

Kitty snorted. "Here and there. I keep alert. Call it self-preservation. The more you know about a person, the better your position is. Information is like gold bullions; it pays for itself."

"Kitty," I said, "you watch too much T.V."

———

The parking lot was packed when we pulled in and we had to park on the road. We left our coats in the cloakroom, which was almost full. A funeral warrants a big turnout. This was a big event.

"I can't help noticing you're wearing a red dress," I said to Cora Mae when she peeled off her black wool coat. "I thought black was your color, and since this is a funeral, it stands to reason you would wear black."

"Not if I want to stand out in a crowd," she replied, squeezing past Kitty. "You don't know anything about snagging a man, do you?"

With Cora Mae in the lead we headed down a short narrow hall to the Green Room, where Chester was laid out. My second hope for the evening—getting a look at Chester—was dashed when I spied the closed casket. My first hope for a lead stood at the head of the casket next to several flower stands, bawling his eyes out.

I headed over, but the room was filled with people I knew and I slowed down to greet them. Most of these people had been at Barney's funeral—Elma and Waino Latvala, the entire Sheedlo family, Lila Carlson, and all of them were hoping for a little extra information about Chester's death. After all, as the sheriff's mother, I might have some extra juicy tidbits to pass around.

I wanted to talk to Chester's son before I shocked everybody with the truth of the matter. "I'm not at liberty to discuss it right now," I told each of them.

People buzzed around, spreading my mysterious comment to those who hadn't heard. Kitty piped up and said, "You're causing quite a stir."

"I hate it when I do that."

By the time I finished fending people off, Bill Lampi wasn't hiding out behind the flower arrangements any more. I looked around for him.

I saw Onni Maki slither by. He grinned like a cat that had just swallowed the canary. He wore a green suit that matched the walls of the room, a paisley shirt, and a thick gold chain around his neck. His thinning hair was wrapped around the top of his head to hide a large bald spot, and when he swept his hand through his hair to make sure it was in place, I noticed a gold ring on his pinky finger.

Cora Mae was gaining on him from behind, her Wonderbra pointing the way. She had a grin on her face, too, like a timber wolf closing in on a bunny rabbit.

I wasn't sure which one to feel sorrier for.

Ed Lacken, the funeral director, stood by the door, looking stiff and proper, his face pinched and red like his bow tie was on too tight.

I poured pink punch into a paper cup and wandered into the bathroom. I set the punch on the sink and went into a stall. I needed to be alone.

Barney had died fourteen months, ten days, and sixteen hours ago, and standing in the funeral home remembering his funeral brought back some of the pain I was trying to forget.

My sad secret—that Barney hadn't really died of a heart attack like I'd told everyone at his funeral—weighed heavily on my heart. The few people who knew the truth, Cora Mae, Blaze, and the funeral director, were sworn to secrecy. It's the way he would have wanted it.

The truth is, Barney drowned in his waders. He went out trout fishing on the Escanaba River, and his body was found floating downstream six hours later. He must have stepped into a deep hole, the waders filled up with water, and he sunk like a boat anchor.

After discussing it with Blaze, we decided Barney wouldn't have wanted people to know he went that way. Sure, he was doing what he loved, but he also prided himself on his outdoor skills, and stepping in a hole wasn't a dignified way to end a great fishing career. Barney would have considered stepping in a hole a stupid thing to do.

I've relived what I imagine were the last few minutes of his life over and over and over again, and I was trying not to go there right now.

I gave myself a few minutes, then splashed cold water on my face and rejoined the group.

Bill Lampi, dwarfed by the flower arrangements, stood alone at the foot of the casket, so I hurried over.

He was a small man, about five foot five, wasted-away thin like he had chronic wasting disease. A pair of oversized coke-bottle glasses magnified his eyes so they appeared owlish, three times larger than they really were. He wasn't big and strapping like most Finns.

I offered my sympathies to him, and he broke down. He didn't take his glasses off, just wiped the tears away as they slid through the frames. His father obviously meant a lot to him.

I put a hand on his bony shoulder and said, "I'm going to do everything I can to catch the maniac who did this and bring him to justice."

Bill Lampi continued to cry until his brain processed my comment, then he stiffened and abruptly quit crying. "What do you mean?"

"I mean whoever killed your father is going to be sorry. I'm after him."

"There was no suggestion of foul play. No one told me Pa was murdered." His voice was shrilling up, hitting high notes. "Was Pa murdered?"

A tall blonde with legs that ended pretty near up to my neck appeared from nowhere and wrapped her arms around Bill. His face slid into her cleavage, which was monumental. All I could think was, wait till Cora Mae gets a load of this. Cat fight for sure.

She turned to me. "I'm Bill's wife, and I want to know what you think you're doing?" In spite of a soft southern lilt, she managed to give the words a frosty northern edge.

Friendly would not be the word that came to mind if I had to describe her. "Just offering my condolences to the family," I said.

"Oh, Barb," Bill's voice was muffled down in the valley. He raised his head and bellowed, "She says Pa was murdered."

The room went dead quiet, starting with the Elma and Waino Latvala corner of the room because that group had been eavesdropping on me all night. It spread like a wave. Waino stuck one finger in his ear and with a turning motion adjusted the volume on his hearing aid.

"Your pa wasn't murdered, sweetheart," She said, warning me with eyes as cold as icicles. "Just an old lady, probably senile, trying to make trouble where there isn't any. Don't you pay any attention."

I studied Barb. She was a beaut for around here, if you like obvious dye jobs and makeup plastered on with a trowel. Apparently most of the men in the room did, because I began noticing the entire room was craning one giant neck in our direction, and the men weren't looking at me.

Blaze pushed through the crowded room, scowling as usual, the smell of his cheap cologne swirling around him.

"Figures you're involved," he said. He took my elbow and moved me away.

Looking back, I saw Barb watching me. If looks could kill, I'd be six feet under. Then the voices started up again, louder than before, filling the room with speculation and anticipation. This was bigger than any of them could have ever hoped for. The phone lines would be burning up tomorrow.

Ed Lacken came by before Blaze could chew me out and asked us to take our seats for the service. I wanted to sit up front because I had a speech to make, but Blaze had a grip on me that I couldn't shake. "The front's for family," he said. "You sit here." He pointed to an empty seat next to Little Donny. Sitting behind me, Cora Mae swiveled her body in Onni's direction. Kitty took up two seats, her legs spread wide.

Ed Lacken started out by saying what a fine man Chester had been and what a loss to the community. Then he asked if anyone wanted to say a piece. Floyd rose from his seat with his bible and headed up.

Great. A sermon.

"Chester was a God-fearing, law-abiding, upstanding family man," he thundered. "And we should all be proud we got to know him."

As far as I knew, Chester hadn't been to church once in his whole life. If he had a relationship at all with God, he kept it to himself. As far as law-abiding went, he made moonshine in his cellar and sold it to the neighbors, and spit on the federal government and its interfering ways just like the rest of us. I wasn't sure about the family man part; Floyd may have got that right.

Floyd paused with an arm raised to the heavens and shouted to the funeral director. "How much time I got to say my piece?"

"Whatever you need." Ed shouted back at him because everyone knows what a defective hearing aid Floyd wears. Personally I think if he'd remember to change the batteries, he'd be fine.

Floyd blah-blahed until I feared he'd never shut up, but eventually he sat down with a winded huff.

I glanced over my shoulder searching for Blaze. Cora Mae and Kitty turned around to see what I was looking at. Blaze, standing in the doorway, seemed in deep conversation with someone in the hall so I trotted up to the front.

"I didn't know Chester all that well," I began. I needed to talk fast to get it out before Raging Bull could react. Out of the corner of my eye, I saw him snorting his way down the aisle. "But I know he didn't deserve what he got, and I know he wasn't shot with God's gold bullet like Floyd thinks. He . . ."

". . . will be sorely missed," Blaze finished for me, arriving at my side.

"I'm not quite done," I whispered to him.

Blaze grinned out at the crowd. Through clenched teeth he said, "Ma, you're done."

"Thank you," I said to the crowd and walked back to my seat as gracefully as possible considering Blaze's arm grip.

"That sure was a fine funeral," I said after the service as Blaze helped me into my coat. Everyone was milling around drinking coffee and eating ginger cookies. "I'd like to stay a little longer."

"I'm putting you out in the truck while I round up your partners in crime. Thanks to you I'll be working overtime tonight."

"Doing what?"

"Damage control."

———

Blaze found Cora Mae and Kitty, loaded them into the truck, and planted himself well away from the side of the truck until I pulled onto the road. He didn't say a word about my driving, which was a relief.

"Is his hand on his gun?" Cora Mae asked, squinting to see in the dark. "He looks like he's ready to draw and fire."

I leaned around Cora Mae to take a look. "Showing off, I guess." Leaning back I said, "I didn't get to talk to Bill Lampi long enough to find out anything. Blaze comes along every time I'm getting somewhere and ruins it. Did you get a load of Bill's wife?"

"Sure did," Cora Mae said. "She's wearing falsies. I'm sure of it."

"I didn't think to look. Leave it to you to latch on to the important things." If Cora Mae's eye for detail extended past the subjects of sex and lust, she'd be an integral part of our investigation team. I'd have to work on developing it.

"Do you know anything about her at all?" I wanted to know. "I mean, besides the falsie thing."

Kitty leaned into the center of the truck cab, scrunching Cora Mae over into the steering wheel. It was all I could do to keep the truck on the road.

"Bill got her a job over at the Highway Department where he works," Kitty said. "She's the one waves the little flag at cars when they're doing road construction. Guys can't keep their minds on work, I hear. I can't understand a thing she says. That southern accent, you know."

"Changing the subject," Cora Mae continued, "guess who has a date for next Tuesday night with yours truly?"

"Got him, hunh?"

"Piece of cake. Onni didn't stand a chance. He's coming to my place and I'm going to make him something to eat and we're going to rent a movie."

"Sounds like a cheap date to me. I'd make him take you out," Kitty suggested. She shifted her hips and everyone in the truck had to readjust. "Either of you have anything for my rummage sale?" she asked.

"Who has a rummage sale in November? That's what I want to know," Cora Mae said.

"I'm desperate for cash. It's the only way of making some quick. You know I lost my job. Gertie, did you put together a few boxes like you said you would?"

"They're in the shed, mostly books, odds and ends. I'll drop the stuff off."

Then I told them about Blaze and the guardianship hearing. I remembered too late that Kitty is Stonely's walking newspaper and there's no way this isn't going to be all over town.

"Impose harm on others?" Kitty hooted. "Where is he coming up with that?"

Cora Mae was angry. "How your own son who lives on your land free could do this . . . makes me glad I never had kids."

Friends are wonderful. They always stick up for you and say just the right things. Sharing my problems with them made me feel better instantly.

"We have to fix you up before you go to court," Cora Mae continued.

"What needs fixing up? I'm fine just the way I am."

"Oh, Gertie, you're a little . . ." Cora Mae was struggling for the right word.

"A little what?" I wanted to know.

"Aggressive."

"Aggressive!" I shouted. "What's that supposed to mean? I've never been aggressive a day in my life."

"Keep your eyes on the road."

What do you think, Kitty? Am I aggressive?"

"Nothing's wrong with being outspoken," Kitty said. I glanced across Cora Mae and saw Kitty's pin-curl-less corkscrews bobbing.

"But you need a wardrobe overhaul," Kitty added.

"Something soft and pink with ruffles to wear to court," Cora Mae agreed.

"I'll eat rabbit pellets before you get me into something pink with ruffles," I said.

I dropped Cora Mae off first. As soon as she slammed the truck door and walked away, Kitty said, "I know why you did that back there."

"What? Back where?" I turned around and looked out the back window of the truck.

"The scene you made with Chester's son. I think you did that on purpose."

I opened my eyes wide in mock surprise. "Now why would I do that?"

"Maybe to flush out the murderer. You think he'll sit tight as long as everyone thinks it was an accident. You think if he knows you're starting to nose around, he might get scared and do something foolish."

"A picayune act," I said, pleased I had found an opportunity to use my new word.

"On the contrary," Kitty said. "It was a fulgent act and very apropos considering the circumstances."

I stared at her. She didn't seem to notice. Fulgent? I cleared my throat. "Do you think he was murdered, too?"

"Probably not, but I'd really like to ride with you."

"Ride with me?"

"I hear you and Cora Mae are starting an investigation business and I'd like to join."

I thought about having to stuff Kitty into the cab of my truck every time we went to interrogate a suspect. A private eye has to blend into the woodwork. Kitty is like a semi coming down a logging road with the logs flying off the back end. You can't miss her.

"I'll think about it, but this isn't a club," I said in my least aggressive tone of voice. "You can't just join anytime you want to."

Besides, I didn't want to have to start carrying a dictionary around with me. Show off.

FIVE

Word for the Day
IMPETUOUS (im PECH oo uhs) adj.
Acting suddenly with little thought;
impulsive.

EVEN THOUGH I WAS angry at Blaze and looking for the right time to talk to him about the whole incompetence court thing, I still was capable of worrying about him. His color wasn't good these days—his face resembled an overripe tomato, and his breathing seemed labored like he'd just run five miles. It could be all that weight he carried. I decided to talk to him soon. A little dieting wouldn't hurt, and he should get a physical to make sure the old thumper operated smoothly.

Maybe he had a medical condition that caused him to behave irrationally, which would explain the court hearing. Or maybe it was the stress of his job.

I wanted to make things right with him. The constant feuding wore me down and interfered with my effectiveness as an investigator. I wanted a truce and I wanted the hearing cancelled, and I knew just how to do it.

He and Mary always go into Trenary for breakfast on Saturdays at Buck's Inn with some of their friends.

Bright and early I drove to Ray's General Store and stocked up on a few supplies I knew I'd need. Then I watched out the window for Blaze's blue Oldsmobile, which is the family car he drives when he isn't on duty. My kids, both Blaze and Star, have to drive right past my house to get out to the road, which as I've mentioned is convenient for keeping an eye on them. I walked out on the porch and waved when Blaze and Mary went by, then ran for Barney's truck.

I pulled into Blaze's drive and parked in front of his mobile home. His sheriff truck was parked in the pole barn, the barn door wide open, inviting me in. I pulled out a can of spray paint from the hardware store and compared the yellow can cover to the color of Blaze's rusted-out sheriff's truck.

Close enough, I thought, and began spraying.

It was colder outside than the can recommended for use, so I had to warm it inside my jacket every once in a while, and I had to keep shaking it as I worked. I only intended to spray the rusted-out areas, but the color match wasn't as good as I'd originally thought and I ended up spraying the entire truck.

It seemed like a good idea at first and I implemented it with the best of intentions. I really thought I could spot-paint the rust spots and make his truck look like new. I really did. But things got out of hand and every over-spray I tried to correct spread like an oil spill on Lake Michigan.

I finished up with a sigh of frustration, my arms sore, my spirits dampened. I'd almost shaken my uppers loose in my mouth.

I couldn't find any masking tape in the barn to cover the silver trim and door handles, which turned out to be a problem. They now were yellow. I had protected the windows as I sprayed by holding up a piece of cardboard I'd ripped from a box. I took a can of paint thinner from a shelf and dabbed with a rag at a few yellow splatters on the window glass.

When I left the barn the ground had a light dusting of fresh snow, like powdered sugar on a doughnut hole. The sun peeked out of the clouds, reflecting off the snow. I dug in my pocket for my Blue Blocker sunglasses and put them on. I leaned against the barn, breathing the fresh air. In the shadow I cast on the side of the barn, I could see my earflaps, and they looked like bird wings poised for flight. I bobbed up and down, pretending I was an eagle. That's where I stood, my earflaps flapping, my sunglasses shielding me from the sun, an empty can of yellow spray paint in my hand, when Blaze and Mary pulled up.

Next time I come back to this world, I plan on coming back as a bird. I'd be safely overhead right now if I could fly. Instead, feeling awkward and helpless, I prepared to "wing it" the only way I knew how.

I grinned.

Glancing down, I saw flecks of yellow paint on the ground circling my feet.

Mary sat closest to me and I could see the look of surprise on her face when she spotted the paint can. Blaze jumped out and, following the paint splotches, ran to the barn door. He was that same overripe tomato color I worried about. He didn't say anything, just turned and walked quickly to the house, his fist clutching his chest.

"I can explain this," I said to Mary when she got out of the car.

"Whatever possessed you to spray paint Blaze's truck?" Mary asked, peering into the barn.

"I'm trying to get on Blaze's good side," I said. "I'm tired of squabbling with him and thought fixing his truck might help. It didn't turn out quite like I expected, though."

Mary covered her mouth with her hand, and I could see the beginning of a smile under it.

"That's so nice of you," Mary said. She walked around the truck with me, checking out my work. "I'd invite you in for coffee," she said, "but let's give Blaze some time."

"That's okay. We all know he's high-strung. I'll take a rain check."

I practically flew out of there even without wings.

———

While I was pulling off my boots on the hall rug, the telephone rang. It rang four times before I got the boots off and could pick up the receiver.

"Better keep your nose in your own backyard," a voice said. "Unless you're looking to have it cut off."

"Who is this?"

I had to wait for an answer because the caller went into a coughing jag—dry, racking coughs only smoking several tons of cigarettes can produce.

"Better pay attention," he hacked. "You ain't getting another chance. Next time, you'll be swimming with the fishes."

"You must have the wrong number," I said, and hung up the phone with a shaking hand.

———

I went over the conversation in my head a million times before I called Cora Mae.

"Settle down," she said. "It was only a crank call."

"The mob's after me."

"The mob?"

"Who else would threaten to throw me to the fishes? Only gangsters talk like that."

"Someone's acting tough. There aren't any gangs in the U.P. This isn't Detroit."

"Maybe you're right," I said. "My nerves aren't as good as they used to be."

My understatement for the day.

———

I'm convinced the section of the Escanaba River west of Perkins is the most beautiful spot in the world. It's hidden from the road so finding it isn't easy if you don't know where to look. I parked the truck by the side of the guardrail, walked over to the top of the path, and peered down. What a sight to behold!

From my position high above the riverbed, angular rocks sprouted up in the river, waterfalls cascaded down steep banks on both sides, and as far as I looked in every direction, there wasn't a human being to be seen.

I crawled down a steep embankment, clutching small tree branches and brush to slow my descent. Soon I was standing next to the rushing water of the great trout river.

Barney fished for trout with a simple rod and reel and a spinner; he didn't need a fancy fly outfit. We pan-fried rainbows and brown trout several times each week from the time the kids were little until Barney passed on last year. Trout fishing was his favorite thing to do.

The Escanaba River appears to be shallow. I've walked out to the middle in spots, sometimes even crossed over to the other side, being very careful. But the rocks are slippery, the current is fast, and the drop-offs are invisible.

Barney wasn't the first and he won't be the last to make a false step and pay the price to the Escanaba River.

I hadn't been back to this spot for years, but in my younger days he and I stood together in waders knee-high in the cold water with the current sweeping past our legs, casting high and wide, the lines glistening in the rising sun, and there wasn't anything better in the whole wide world.

Sitting on a flat rock on the side of the river, I talked to Barney. All the while, I had the feeling that he was watching me, looking down from above. I searched the sky. Nothing but clouds.

I explained to Barney that it was taking me a great deal of time to adjust to the idea that he was gone, and now with this phone conversation, things weren't going so well, and he should give me a sign that things would be okay. Any sign would do.

I sat waiting a long time, but no sign came, although I still felt a watchful gaze upon me.

As I struggled up the steep slope, I heard a car door slam, and as I crested the hill, I spotted the back end of a magenta-colored sedan round the bend and disappear.

———

When I returned home, Carl and Little Donny had finished hunting for the day and invited me for a quick one. We piled into what was left of Carl's station wagon and headed over to Herb's Bar. By this time I needed a quick one the size of a gallon pitcher.

I glanced around the interior of Carl's car. It needed work after the deer attack, but Little Donny had agreed to pay for the damage without involving the insurance company. That way Carl's insurance premiums wouldn't go up and it kept Carl happy.

Herb's Bar is the only bar within twenty square miles and is owned by Star's twins, Ed and Red. I can't say why the bar was ever called Herb's because, thinking back, no one by the name of Herb ever owned it, at least not in my time. And I've been around a spell.

When Little Donny opened the door, the whole place quieted down. You could have heard a nickel drop behind the bar. That's small-town life in the U.P. Everyone stopped talking and turned to see who was coming in. Nobody called out a greeting until they looked past Little Donny and saw Carl and me. By the time Carl shut the door, everybody was back to his own business.

The place sure was hopping. Carl found one bar stool at the far end of the bar and helped me crawl up onto it. We had to wait a few minutes until Red worked his way down to us. Little Donny and Carl ordered tap beer. I settled for a soda pop.

The twins looked exactly alike from the day they were born, and still do. The only thing that saves me from total confusion is their hair. Once the baby hair fell out, Ed's came in chestnut-colored like the horse I had my eye on long ago. Red's came in the color of fresh-pulled carrots. His birth name was Ned, but we just naturally started calling him Red, and the name stuck. A lot of discussion ensued about where that red hair came from, but if I recall right, my own German Nana had fiery red hair.

The twins are in their early twenties, slender like marsh reeds, and are handsome pups. They share a two-bedroom apartment above the bar, and I hear they're hot with the local girls. They're hard workers though—have to give them credit where credit's due. Finns and Swedes admire hard workers.

"Sorry we had to miss dinner the other night," Red shouted over the noise, "but since hunting season started, we've been working 'round the clock."

"You missed Chester's funeral yesterday," I shouted back. "I'm investigating his death, you know."

Before Red could reply, an out-of-town hunter stomped his empty glass on the counter and Red hurried away.

Carl, Little Donny, and I toasted to Little Donny's future hunting success, which I was losing faith in, and we downed our drinks.

I'd never seen Herb's Bar so busy. Every hunter from across the county must be pounding them back tonight. My eyes swept up and down the bar. I turned to the tables and studied each of the hunters sitting down.

I remembered the threatening phone call and the smoker's cough. Was he in here right this minute—and which one would he be? Was Chester's killer sitting right next to me while I sipped my soda?

I lifted my glass to my lips and my eyes locked with a grubby-looking guy at the other end of the bar, which wasn't anything unusual. Most of the hunters in Herb's are grubby. Part of the attraction of hunting for the men is the length of time they get to take between showers and shaves. Being a dirtball is expected and welcome behavior.

Only this guy was different. He looked like he should be on the Most Wanted list at the post office. In some ways he looked pretty much like everyone else in the bar—scruffy, several days' growth on his face, greasy unwashed hair poking out of a dirty gray ball cap. The difference was in his eyes. They radiated pure evil, cold and hateful, and they were glaring right at me.

I looked away first and shivered. Suddenly, I felt cold.

"Who's that guy at the end of the bar?" I said to Ed when I was sure he wasn't watching.

Ed shrugged. "Don't know."

"Is he from around here?"

"Don't think so. I've only seen him this week."

I glanced across the bar and watched him paying up with Red. He looked back at me one last time before leaving, with cold dark eyes and a cigarette hanging from his lips.

Cora Mae opened her front door before I crawled out of my truck, a cup of coffee in her hand.

"You won't sleep tonight," I warned, refusing a cup.

"What brings you by so late?"

I told my best friend about the car following me at the river and about the sinister man at the bar. "He stared me down."

"You mean he won."

"I had to look away. He gave me the creeps." I shivered, thinking about it.

"Did you recognize the car?"

"No. Who around here owns a purple car?"

"Nobody that I know." Cora Mae sipped her coffee. "We'll keep a lookout. By the way, Kitty stopped by earlier. She brought over an application."

"An application for what?"

"She's applying for a job with us as an investigator."

"This is a nonpaying job. Does she know that?"

"I told her we couldn't pay her, and she said that's okay. Her unemployment will start up in a little while and she's getting ready for her rummage sale. She says this job has future monetary possibilities like one of those new stock market companies. An IOP."

"It's IPO, Cora Mae—initial public offering."

I picked up Kitty's résumé, which was lying on the table. It was neatly typed, but the ink was faded and the corners were crumpled.

"She said it needs updating," Cora Mae explained.

"I'll say." I noted her height at five-foot-four and her weight at one hundred and thirty-two pounds. "First off, no one puts their height and weight on a job application, and second off, Kitty hasn't weighed one hundred and thirty-two pounds since she was four years old. What do you think about working with her?"

"Me? Doesn't matter to me. The business was your idea and you can run it any way you want. There's something about her that bothers me, though, but I can't put my finger on it."

"She stands too close when she's talking to you," I guessed.

"That's it! That's exactly it."

Kitty stands about a foot closer to your face than you really feel comfortable with, and backing up doesn't do a bit of good; she follows right over. Her comfort zone is way different than the rest of the world's.

Cora Mae shrugged. "She says she'd be an asset."

"I don't like the idea at all," I said.

"Well, she said think about it."

I thought about it for two seconds. Life was complicated enough without Kitty in the mix. I had my hands full with my own family, especially Blaze and Grandma Johnson.

And with whoever was following and threatening me.

SIX

Word for the Day
MALAISE (ma LAYZ) n.
A vague feeling of physical discomfort
or uneasiness.

MOST OF THE SNOW had melted on Saturday, but by Sunday morning a cold snap settled in and the remaining snow turned to ice. I wrapped a scarf around my face and started the truck. The ice on the windshield peeled off in sheets under the blade of my scraper.

I hustled inside and while the truck warmed up, I called Blaze.

"I want you to stop this court thing right now," I said without bothering with any small talk first. "I'm a busy woman. I don't have time for this."

"I tried to talk to you, but talking to you is like talking to a cement truck."

"If you ever had anything interesting to say, I might listen."

Blaze dropped his voice to a soothing level like he was talking to a child or to someone who is deranged. He sounded patronizing and false. "You haven't been yourself since Pa died. I'm worried about you and just want to help."

"So you want a court to say I'm incompetent to manage my own affairs and that I'm a danger to society. That's how you want to help?"

"Be reasonable," he said. "You run around thinking everyone's been murdered, you spray painted my truck yellow, and—and this is the best one—the bank says you took all the money you and pa saved out of the bank in a paper bag. Where's all the money, ma?"

"None of your business."

"If you tell me where the money is and let me help you manage it, I'll drop the hearing."

"See you in court," I said before slamming down the receiver.

———

Cora Mae came out to the truck when I pulled up. She had on a black pillbox hat and dangly black earrings. She was wrapped in black fake fur.

I looked her over. I wore snow bibs under my hunting jacket, Blue Blockers to cut the glare of winter sun on snow, my hunting cap with the flaps down, and snowmobile mittens.

"This isn't church we're going to," I said. "You never know where an investigator's work will take her. We might have to track someone through the woods. A near-sighted hunter is going to think you're a bear and that'll be the end of you."

"I always dress up to go calling." Cora Mae looked me over. "And it wouldn't hurt you once in a while. We talked about the way you dress yesterday. If you want to make a good impression in court, you better change your attire soon."

I decided not to tell her about my conversation with Blaze. My best friend might agree with him.

We drove over to the far side of Stonely without incident, unless you count the dip into the ditch when I over-steered pulling onto Crevit Road and lost control.

I backed easily, if not exactly straight, out of the ditch and glanced at Cora Mae. She straightened her pillbox hat and cleared her throat. "That was a tricky corner," she said.

We pulled up in front of a house shingled with asphalt roofing tiles that were peeling loose. A Toyota sat in the driveway, which I figured must belong to Barb, since no one from around here would ever buy a foreign car. Detroit's reputation as the capital of car country has nothing to do with it. It's leftover bad feelings from World War II. Stonely folks drive Fords, sometimes GMs, but never a Japanese car or a German car. Grandma Johnson says, "Remember Pearl Harbor?" She checks labels and tags before buying clothes so she doesn't accidentally buy something made in Japan. "Remember Hitler? No one in this family better ever buy a Kraut car," she says.

She always looks me straight in the eye when she talks about Hitler, like he was my fault. At least she hasn't called me a Kraut right to my face. Although she serves me sauerkraut every chance she gets.

Barb Lampi answered the door in a pink robe, her hair uncombed and makeup smeared around the bottom of her eyes, but she woke up fast when she saw me.

"Yes?" Her tone sounded suspicious, her speech thick and slow in that Southern manner.

"We came to pay our respects," I said, waving to include Cora Mae.

Barb eyed Cora Mae up and down, and Cora Mae eyed her back, and I could feel the sparks boomeranging and whizzing overhead.

"Well, you've paid them," she said and began to close the door.

I stuck my boot in the doorjamb and called out, "Wait a minute, there. We need to ask Bill a few questions."

Barb leaned on the door, trying to close it. "Like what kind of questions?"

"I'm investigating his father's murder. I need his help."

Barb opened the door, and, caught off-guard, I almost fell in. She wrapped her fist around my arm and squeezed, and I could feel the muscle in her grip, the surprising strength.

"Listen, you busybody," she said. "Get off my porch and don't come back."

"Or?" I asked. It appeared to me that I was being threatened, a daily occurrence lately. Barb's throaty voice reminded me of a smoker. I sniffed her robe and thought I detected stale smoke.

"Or I'll call Sheriff Johnson to come and get you." Barb still had my arm and twisted it, forcing me to step back out on the porch. I hoped I didn't embarrass myself by dropping to my knees.

"What's the trouble?" I heard from inside the house.

"Nothing at all. Just a saleswoman and she's leaving." Barb released my arm.

"Bill," I called out. "I'd like to have a word with you."

"I'm calling the sheriff." And Barb shut the door.

"Did you see that?" I said to Cora Mae when we were back in the truck. "She assaulted me. And where were you when I needed help?"

"You looked like you were handling things just fine."

I huffed. "We're going to have to tackle this problem from a different angle."

"I can't believe you stuck your foot in the door like that," Cora Mae said. "That was aggressive behavior, exactly what you're supposed to be working on controlling. I'm just pointing it out to you."

"Cora Mae, an investigator has to do what needs to be done."

"Just pointing it out."

———

We had time to kill, since our visit with the Lampis was cut short. Cora Mae wanted to go to the cemetery to check on the graves of her three dead husbands, all buried in a family plot Cora Mae bought right before husband number one hit the dirt. She bought four plots, thinking maybe they would have children and eventually might like to be buried together. One big happy family.

But Cora Mae never had children and she loaded up three of the gravesites with dead husbands. Life turns out funny. Not ha ha funny—funny as in sad and unexpected.

Stonely doesn't have a cemetery. You have to go to Escanaba or Trenary to rest in eternity. Most folks around here prefer the Trenary cemetery because it's closer, and because nobody cares what you put on the graves for decorations. The Escanaba cemetery is fussy, and they'll yank off whatever you put down as soon as your back is turned.

When I go, I want to be gussied up in my old hunting jacket and cap for a showing at Lacken's Funeral Home, and I hope the whole county comes and gets good and drunk afterwards at Herb's Bar. Then I want to be cremated and have part of my ashes buried with Barney and half scattered to the wind on Bear Creek behind my house.

When I told Blaze my plan, he said it was against the law to scatter ashes. Littering, he called it, in his righteous sheriff voice. Cora Mae and Star know what I want, and it's going to be done like I say. I even wrote my request down, had it witnessed by Cora Mae and Star, and Cora Mae locked it in her safe deposit box.

Of course, those plans are a long way off.

I miss Barney so much, I thought to myself as we headed toward the cemetery. A car approached and Cora Mae waved.

"Who was that?" I asked, snapping out of my daydream.

"Bill Lampi."

"The same Bill Lampi we just left?" I screamed.

Cora Mae was almost launched from the truck when I slammed on the brakes and accomplished a perfect U-turn.

"Hold your hat," I called to her. "Who was Barb talking to back at the house if Bill wasn't home?"

Cora Mae didn't answer. She clutched the dashboard as I slammed on the brakes again. I couldn't believe my eyes.

The magenta sedan, the same purple car that had spied on me at the river, streaked past us heading the opposite way.

"That's the car," I shouted. "The one that followed me to the river."

I didn't know which car to follow.

I made a quick decision and swung around again to pursue the purple car. My U-turn wasn't quite as perfect this time.

Cora Mae screamed as we headed for the ditch.

———

"There's a piece of barbed wire stuck on your front bumper," Little Donny said when I pulled into the drive. He was headed to the shed with George, but he stopped and removed the wire.

"Can't imagine where that came from," I lied.

"Gonna help George," Little Donny said. "Grandma Johnson's in the house."

"How'd she get here?"

"Blaze dropped her off."

The battle between Blaze and me was only in the second round, and already he was hitting below the belt.

The house smelled like old-lady-dried-out-prune-skin odor hiding out under cheap flowery perfume. From the smell of the house, Grandma Johnson had been waiting a while.

"Where you been while I been sittin' here all day?"

"I went visiting with Cora Mae. You should have told me you were coming."

"Didn't know I was coming," Grandma huffed. She was sitting in the rocker with her arms folded across her chest, her face scrunched like she was sucking on a lemon. "Blaze just dumped me off."

I sat down and looked helplessly at the woman with the snake tongue.

"I'm glad he did," she continued, "because me and you have to have a little talk about your behavior. You're embarrassing our family left and right and we can't stand for it anymore."

"I'm embarrassing the family?" I couldn't believe it. Grandma Johnson's front yard has a toilet filled with plastic flowers, and in her garden are wood-carved people bent over picking vegetables. Their underpants are showing. Grandma would win a most-embarrassing-relative contest hands down.

"Traipsing around with that Cora Mae, who's a disgrace to Stonely, and causing all kinds of commotion. I hear that poor deceased man's son and daughter-in-law were attacked right there at the funeral home by 'that orange-headed woman.' Who ya suppose they were talking about?"

I touched my hair with my hand. I was getting used to my orange curls and toyed with the idea of keeping the color, if for no other reasons than to annoy certain relatives.

Grandma Johnson went on and on, and after awhile I managed to tune her out without her knowing what I was doing. Outside, a squirrel intent on stealing every last kernel of birdseed in the feeder made six trips back and forth carrying seed away before Grandma ran down. I hope I learn to shut up better when I'm ninety-two.

I excused myself, found Little Donny in the barn, and informed him that Grandma Johnson could be taken home, and right now. I would have liked to stay out there and talk to George awhile, but in my hurry to get away from Grandma, I had run outside without my jacket, and I was freezing.

"I enjoyed our little talk," Grandma Johnson said while Little Donny helped her to the truck. "Maybe we should make a point of doin' this every Sunday. Sorry our visit was cut short on account of you feeling under the weather."

"Malaise," I muttered under my breath using my word for the day.

"What do you mean 'my legs'? If your legs hurt so much, you better take an aspirin." She peered into my eyes. "You don't look so good. Worse than usual even."

As I watched Little Donny and Grandma Johnson pull away, I had a face twitch I couldn't control.

After I slipped into my jacket I took a jar of Vaseline out to the birdfeeder and greased up the pole real good. There's nothing I hate more than squirrels stealing bird food. Raccoons and grackles are right up at the top of my list too, but squirrels are the worst nuisances.

I filled up the feeder, then sat at the window to watch two of the little rodents take turns jumping up and sliding down the pole. When a squirrel clamps onto an idea, he never quits. They must have slid back down that pole ten or twelve times until the Vaseline wore away. Then, triumphantly, one sat on top of the feeder stuffing his face and grinning at me.

At dusk, Little Donny came in from the blind, deerless again. Trailing him by a few minutes, George arrived, looking dapper in his tight-fitting jeans, blue flannel shirt, and snake-trimmed hat.

"Joining us for poker?" he asked me, while Little Donny wolfed down half of a pot roast and three pounds of mashed potatoes.

"Whose house this week?"

"Blaze's."

"He and I aren't getting along. Think I'll pass." I watched Little Donny dip into the apple pie.

"Since when did you two ever get along, and since when has it ever kept you away from a good card game?" George tilted his hat back before delivering his challenge. "You're letting him win."

That did it. George had a point. Why should I let Blaze drive me away?

Which reminded me of my off-the-road experience and the two cars that escaped. I couldn't believe my bad luck. I touched my tender temple lightly with my fingers. I never realized before that driving was hazardous to your health. I'd have to call Cora Mae later and check on that knee she banged up.

"Count me in," I said to George. "But poker isn't my game."

———

"Rummy," I said to the group, fanning my last cards across the table and grinning. "That's it. I won again."

Little Donny counted his cards. George shoved back in his chair and stretched his legs. Sourpuss Blaze scowled and studied the cards.

"I called no cheating, Ma. At the beginning of the game."

Sometimes, just for fun when the kids were young, we would allow cheating. It had to be called at the beginning of the game, agreed on by all players, and you lost points if you were caught. I miss those days.

"I heard you call it."

"Then why," Blaze said, "is the last card you played from another deck of cards." He reached over and turned the card over. Sure enough, it didn't match the other deck. "I can't believe you cheated."

"Don't know how that card got in there," I lied.

"Have you been cheating from the start?"

"Yup," George said, grinning at me.

"Well if you knew it all along, why didn't you tell us?" Blaze complained to George.

"I'm through playing." I gathered the cards in front of me into a neat pile. "Go ahead and play poker. I'm walking home."

"I'll drop you off," George offered. "It's pretty dark out."

"I think I can manage to make it down the road without help. I've been walking this road my entire life and I need the exercise." The spare tire around my middle needed some work.

Swinging a flashlight ahead of me, I walked through the brisk night air enjoying the sounds of nature. A pack of coyotes howled in the distance. An animal scampered across the road beyond the beam of the flashlight, and I could smell fallen leaves, oaks and maples, crunching underfoot.

I sensed something wrong when I put my foot on the first porch step. I knew for sure something was wrong when I opened the door and saw the destruction. What I didn't know for sure was whether or not the intruder was still inside.

Fear rippled up and down my spine as I backed quietly down the steps and stumbled through the dark toward the safety of Blaze's home.

SEVEN

Word for the Day
DINT (dint) n.
Force; exertion.

COLORED LIGHTS FROM BLAZE's truck streaked through the night and the sound of the siren pierced the air. I couldn't help wondering if stealth on our part might have been a better way to go. Why does law enforcement always have to warn the world they are coming? Doesn't that give the bad guys time to pack up and mosey out?

Blaze and George went in first, guns drawn, cautious. Little Donny and I waited in George's truck, strobe lights slicing through the windshield, exposing our frightened faces. Keeping Little Donny inside the truck wasn't an easy task; he wanted to be with the men. But nineteen years old is too young for taking risks, and this was one area Blaze and I finally agreed on. So Little Donny and I sat.

Finally, Blaze and George trudged out, Blaze's weapon holstered, George's rifle pointed into the ground, grim sets to their jaw.

Little Donny and I hurried over. "I'm going in," I said.

George placed a hand on my shoulder. "It'll keep for another day, Gertie. It's a mess in there."

But I had to see for myself.

The devastation was extensive—drawers upended, bedding slashed, lamps smashed, drapes ripped in shreds. The rage it took to accomplish such a violent act frightened me with its intensity.

"Who knew you were out for the evening?" Blaze wanted to know.

It was a good question, one I didn't have an answer to. No one I knew could possibly be capable of such viciousness, such hate.

"Anything missing?" George asked, following me as I wandered, speechless, through the house.

I shook my head, nothing obviously missing. I was fleetingly grateful that I'd buried my money under the apple tree instead of in the box spring, which lay shredded in ribbons.

"No sign of forced entry," Little Donny observed, studying the front door.

"Of course, it wasn't forced. I didn't lock it."

Little Donny lives in a big city where you lock your doors and windows and have security systems tied into the police department. In the U.P. most of us can't remember where we put the key to the door and don't particularly care. The only time we even think about locking up is if we will be out of town for a while and we don't want our friends and family borrowing things without our knowledge.

Blaze, unusually quiet, waited by the door with me. George straightened a chair and scooped pillows from the floor and tossed them on the sofa.

"You okay, Ma?" Blaze took my arm, his voice gentle, and I nodded, resigned. "You can't stay here tonight."

I already knew that, and my choices weren't good. I couldn't go to Star's place. She has cats and I'm deathly allergic to cat dander. Just thinking of going to Grandma Johnson's house made the nerve in my eye start twitching, and I'd rather eat nails than stay with Blaze.

"You take Little Donny with you," I said to Blaze. "I'm going to Cora Mae's."

——

The next morning I showered and wrapped one of Cora Mae's black silk robes around me. She had a pot of coffee ready and was made up for the day, every hair in place, like a soap opera star. I bet she went to bed with her makeup and hair done up. She probably slept on her back with one of those little rolled pillows tucked under her neck and a black mask to screen out light.

I had slept in a tiny spare bedroom on a day bed with a white comforter and ruffles around the bottom. On a shelf above the bed were two porcelain dolls decked out in wedding dresses.

While I sipped coffee I glanced around. Cora Mae lived in a dollhouse. Her home was tiny, but uncluttered and spotlessly clean, and everything was white—white walls, white sofa, white kitchen table. Cora Mae was sheathed in black armor in a pearly white house.

I've known Cora Mae most of my life. Her tastes always ran white; white car, white fence, white rugs. The black clothes are a new addition, which I chalk up to her post-menopause phase.

"What are you going to do, Gert?" she asked. "You can stay here as long as you want, you know that. I have plenty of room."

"Thanks, Cora Mae, but I don't want to put you in danger."

"Danger's my middle name. I thrive on it." Jane Bond put a plate of blueberry pancakes in front of me and I dove in. "Still think it's the mob?" she said between bites.

I shrugged. "It's pretty scary. I can't figure it out. I must be getting too close to Chester's murderer and someone's getting nervous."

"Maybe you should listen to them and back off. It isn't worth getting hurt over."

"We need to stock up on weapons," I said. I refused to let anyone scare me away. "Someone's playing rough. I need to go into Escanaba to the Assessor's office. Then we can shop for ammo."

"Gertie, why are you doing this? Don't you want to hand it over to Blaze?"

"No, I don't. He won't do a good job."

"So you're doing this because you feel you have to?"

"Cora Mae, I'm doing it because I have to have a reason to get up every day. I'm doing it because I'm living alone for the first time in forty-some years and I can't wake up in the morning and get excited about playing cards with the seniors or going to bingo."

Cora Mae, who buried a lot of men and had to get used to living alone more than once, patted my hand and said, "I understand completely."

I looked down at Cora Mae's silk robe. "I need to get dressed," I said.

"Don't put on the same clothes you wore yesterday. I have just the thing, and it'll fit perfectly. I even have shoes for you, so you can get out of those boots."

I scowled and shook my head, but gave in when I saw how disappointed she looked. "Okay," I said, grudgingly.

Cora Mae clapped her hands like a big kid, delighted that she was finally getting the opportunity to dress me.

I squeezed into a pair of black stretch pants, which showed off my thigh lumps. Cora Mae didn't own any flat shoes so I chose a pair of her black boots with the lowest heels and a gray cotton sweater. We found an orange moon necklace that matched my hair and Cora Mae pulled a blue and black plaid three-quarter-length coat out of a back closet.

I looked like I should be on a street corner. I would have changed back into my own clothes but I didn't want to hurt Cora Mae's feelings.

The things we do for our friends.

————

We were in my truck ready to go, when, in the rearview mirror, I spotted the magenta sedan pulling into Cora Mae's driveway.

"Duck, Cora Mae," I warned her, throwing my body across the bench seat and hauling her down. "Shhh . . . it's the car that's been following me. Stay down."

A few minutes later we heard pounding on Cora Mae's kitchen door, and I hazarded a peek out the side window. I jerked up straight, releasing Cora Mae, and jumped out of the truck.

"Kitty, what are you doing?" I demanded.

Startled, Kitty let out a shriek and raised a plump arm to her throat. "Where did you come from? I just walked past your truck and you weren't in it."

Ignoring her question, I pointed to the purple car. "When did you get that?" My eyes sighted down my extended arm and I couldn't help noticing she had a driver along with her. The driver was the same creepy character I'd noticed at the bar. "And who is that?"

"Jeff, get out of the car and come meet my friends," Kitty called out, and he rose out of the car and walked forward, flicking ashes over his shoulder from a cigarette dangling in his fingers. "This is my third cousin on my father's mother's side. He's visiting for hunting season."

Cora Mae slunk into the middle of the group and elbowed me aside. She had on her stalking pose, breasts forward, eyes rolled so the whites of her eyes showed beneath her pupils. I grabbed the back of her coat and pulled. She stumbled back, but didn't break her gaze on Kitty's cousin.

"These two have been following me around," I said to her. "That's the car I spotted at the Escanaba River."

Kitty loomed over us on the porch so I moved slightly away in case she lost her footing and fell. I was directly in line to have the life crushed out of me. I pulled Cora Mae along, too.

Jeff, apparently wanting no part of a confrontation, turned back to the car. "I'll let you work this out. I'll be waiting in the car." Then he coughed.

"That's it," I shouted. "That's the voice of the guy who called my house and threatened to kill me and throw me to the fishes. That's him. Call Blaze, Cora Mae. Go on." I gave her a shove toward the house. Kitty blocked the way.

"Settle down, everybody," she said. "It's not what it looks like. We were trying to help."

"Help what? Help kill me? Go on, Cora Mae. Don't let Kitty stop you. Call for backup."

Kitty spread her legs in a firm stance. Cora Mae looked at each of us, but didn't move.

"We did follow you," Kitty admitted. "It was all my idea. All I want to do is join the team and I thought if I followed you around and figured out what you were up to, I might have a better chance at the job."

"What does he have to do with it?" I pointed at Jeff.

"He drove me around in his car because you would have noticed mine."

"He called and threatened me."

Kitty looked uncomfortable and her eyes shifted to the left. A sure sign she was about to make up something.

"The truth," I insisted.

"Well . . . he did make the call. But only because I told him to. And I'm really sorry. I really am. I figured if you thought you were in danger, you might decide you needed me."

I studied Kitty, and found myself believing her, as incredible as that seemed. What a desperate and lonely woman she must be to go to this extent to be included.

"Wait a minute," I said. "You and your cousin destroyed my house. You broke in and slashed and smashed my things. You went too far. Cora Mae, call for backup."

Kitty's eyes widened, her face the color of silly putty. She shook her head. "Oh no, I'd never do anything to hurt you. Neither would Jeff. Is it true? Did you really have a break-in? Honest, Gertie, you have to believe me."

"You didn't break into my house?"

"Cross my heart and hope to die, I didn't."

A moment or two of silence ensured while I considered Kitty's believability and my options. "I can't pay you," I said.

"I understand and that's okay." A broad smile lit up Kitty's face. "I can work full-time now, but if I get a paying job I'll have to cut back my hours to weekends and nights. You won't regret this, Gertie. When do I start and what do you want me to do?"

"Tell Jeff to take off without you. Starting right now you're my official bodyguard."

Kitty almost fell off the porch. I wasn't there to break her fall, but the bear hug she wrapped around me almost crushed me to death, anyway.

———

"Where are you going?" Cora Mae asked. "Escanaba's the other way."

"Ray's," I said, pulling into the general store's parking lot and parking between the yellow lines. I was getting pretty good at driving. "You coming in?"

"Naw, bring me some chewing gum," she said. "Juicy Fruit."

Kitty grabbed hold of the open door and with a shove from Cora Mae, stood up. I walked past several parked trucks and recognized one as George's. Glancing down at my clothes, I thought about saving this errand till later, but later isn't a word I care for. It's for slackers.

I marched in with my bodyguard in hot pursuit.

Ray's daughter stood at the checkout counter waiting on customers. Ray was in the deli making hot sandwiches, wiping his hands on a stained white apron tied across the bulge of his belly. George lounged against the meat case, wearing his snake hat and a playful attitude.

He whistled when he saw me. "Where you off to today?" He looked me up and down. I hoped Cora Mae's coat was covering most of my bottom. I'd rather keep my fat rolls to myself.

"Not letting the grass grow is all." I tugged at the bottom of the short coat.

"Looks like Cora Mae's been dressing you. That or you're going through some new phase."

"Ray," I said, calling past George and his silly amused grin, "I need to talk to you for a minute." Out of the corner of my eye, I saw Kitty loading up a shopping cart.

"Sure, Gertie." Ray stepped out from behind the counter. "What you need?"

"George tells me Chester was in here last week and I need to know what he bought."

"Everybody in Tamarack County was in here last week, and you want me to remember what one of them bought?"

"Yep."

Ray scratched his chin, thought for a spell, then said, "Don't remember."

"I was in here too," George said to Ray. "Chester had a little bag, like a paper lunch sack, and came out of the back room."

The back room was stocked with hardware and gun supplies. It was the most popular part of the store with the men, a social gathering place where they stretched stories.

"Maybe I do remember." Ray sounded surprised at his own memory. "He bought buckshot, and that seemed funny 'cuz Chester never used buckshot. Buckshot's for folks who can't aim so good, and Chester was the best there was. I kidded with him about it."

Someday when I have time, I'll set Ray straight concerning buckshot, which I use all the time and it isn't because I couldn't shoot straight. It's for better coverage.

"Chester said he didn't want to kill the varmint hanging around pestering him," Ray continued. "He said he wanted to scare it off. And he seemed mad, real mad."

"Chester usually kills an animal if it hangs around too long," George said, adjusting his hat. "He doesn't hesitate, especially if he thinks it might be rabid."

"Maybe when he said varmint," I offered, "he meant something entirely different."

"I have to agree with you, Gertie." Ray ran his hands across the front of his white apron. "He said someone was pestering him, not minding their own business."

"Their own business?" I repeated. "Ray, can you remember exactly what he said? Did he say their own business or his own business?"

Ray scratched his chin. "Don't know."

"Did he say someone wasn't minding her own business?"

"No, I'd remember that."

Ray got testy after I wouldn't let it go. "I don't remember, Gertie, because *I* mind my own business."

Minding your own business is the number one rule if you want to get along in the U.P., or at least appearing as though you're minding it. Busybodies are welcome additions because they bring fresh material into an otherwise routine day, as long as they don't throw their two cents in with it. In other words, gossiping and rumoring are permitted, personal opinionating on the topic of gossip isn't.

"Maybe kids have been hanging around his property or his hunting shack," Ray offered, "and he just wanted to dig up some dirt around their feet. That happened to me once. Kids were sneakin' into my strawberry patch, eatin' my strawberries. I waited around the corner of the house until they showed up. You should'a seen 'em scatter when that shotgun went off."

Ray started laughing and decided the story was funny enough for a second go around. While he was telling it again I wandered off, hunting for Juicy Fruit gum. Ray was still laughing over his story while I paid up.

Kitty was nowhere in sight.

George walked me out to the truck. He grinned when I handed Cora Mae her chewing gum and she squealed. She's like a kid in a candy store.

"Wait up," Kitty called, rounding the corner with a cart bulging with bags. "Thought I'd buy us a few snacks."

"There isn't an inch of extra room up front," I said. "Put them in the back."

I needed Kitty's bodyguarding techniques about as much as I needed a hole in my head, no disrespect intended toward Chester.

———

The ride to Escanaba, forty miles away, took more than an hour. Cars whizzed past, all in a big hurry to get someplace else, and the drivers seemed overly combative. One low-life character even flipped us the raspberry for no good reason.

I tried to stay as far to the right side of the road as I could so the nuts had a lot of passing room. Sixty-five miles an hour seemed unreasonably fast to me so I tried to keep it around forty. You could enjoy the scenery that way.

Since I had a hard time seeing over the dashboard, Cora Mae let me sit on her purse. That made a difference.

Kitty polished off six powdered-sugar doughnuts, leaving most of the sugar on her shelf-like bosom and on Cora Mae's lap. "Who would break into your house?" she wanted to know.

"Same person who broke into Chester's," I said, making a conscious effort to keep my eyes on the road rather than on Kitty's food fest. "Wipe your mouth, Cora Mae. You have sugar everywhere."

"But to slash your furniture and break up things," Kitty continued. "It's a warning. Someone's scared or worried."

My take on the situation exactly.

At the Register of Deeds I had to drive around the block six times before I found an easy place to park. I figure I'm not ready for parallel parking between cars.

Cora Mae swiped powdered sugar from her lap as Kitty headed for the door. I made a feeble attempt to brush the excess from my truck seats.

"No more eating powdered doughnuts in my truck," I called to Kitty's disappearing back, and had to hurry to catch up.

"Howdy." A large, round-faced woman worked a mouth full of gum. "What you need?"

"I'm representing Chester Lampi's family," I said, business-like. "He's dead, and I need to look at his property records. For the family. These are my associates."

"Records are public property. Anyone can look through 'em," she chomped. "We ain't computerized though. There's the books." She waved at a room full of blue bindings. "Help yourself."

It took a while to figure out the filing system, property listings in one section, deeds in another.

"Looky this," Cora Mae shrilled over my shoulder. "This says Onni Maki owns one lousy acre. I didn't think that was possible in Stonely. I'm sure he said he owned a ton of land. This can't be right."

I looked it over. "One acre's what he's got."

"One miserable acre." Cora Mae was obviously disappointed. If she was expecting a hot date *and* wealth she was looking in the wrong town.

"No wonder he's taking Viagra," she said. "Doesn't have anything else going for him."

"Who owns all the woods next to him?" Kitty said from a chair across the table.

"Don't know." I scanned the printout, surprised at what I saw. "It appears that Chester Lampi owns, or owned, the woods."

"No, Chester's place is at least five miles from Onni's."

Getting used to the columns of numbers, I cross-referenced several pages, wrote down a few numbers and added them up. Then walked over to Bubble Gum.

"Could you come and check my numbers," I said. "I must have made a mistake. I need you to tell me."

Cora Mae slumped in her chair as if her ship had just come in and it was filled with cow manure. Bubbles sighed heavily, like I'd interrupted something way more important than this. She got up slowly, walked over to the files, and studied the page. Looking at my chicken scratches, she said, "Nope, you didn't make a mistake. That's right."

"You're telling me that Chester Lampi owned four hundred acres of land around Stonely? And we didn't know about most of it?"

"Yeah," said Bubbles, "but they ain't connected. See, eighty's right here." She pointed to a map on the page.

"That's the two forties he lives on," I pointed out to Cora Mae, who was regaining interest.

"And three hundred and twenty is over here," Bubbles finished.

"Next to Onni." I was talking to myself out loud. "He sure owned a lot of land; a regular land baron."

I mulled over this new information, feeling it was connected somehow. This wasn't exactly prime real estate property on the outskirts of Chicago. It was in God-forsaken country where you can get a lot of land for your buck. Even though four hundred acres is a lot of acres, it shouldn't be worth killing over. I couldn't see Chester's son, or anyone else for that matter, killing him for his land.

Which led me to new questions. Why didn't Bill live on some of this land? Instead he lived on a small patch of his own. I checked the records. Bill Lampi owned the property and house we visited. Forty acres to be exact, and he'd owned it for seven years.

"What's this part of the deed mean?" I asked Bubbles, who was having a bubble-blowing contest with Cora Mae. Cora Mae's Juicy Fruit lost the contest.

Bubbles popped the winning bubble across her face, sucked it in, and studied the document. "Title's not free and clear. Mineral rights are owned by someone else."

"Who owns them?"

"You have to look in that other book."

I opened another thick binder and paged through. "I need help. I can't find it."

Bubbles sighed heavily and found the page for me. "Onni Maki owns the mineral rights to Chester's land," I muttered out loud.

Kitty leaned over the table. "That's odd. Chester owns the land and Onni owns the mineral rights? How did that happen?"

"I'd like to know that, too," I said. "Cora Mae, your date with Onni's tomorrow. You have to pump him for information."

Cora Mae groaned. "I'm not interested in Onni anymore."

"It's not all rich rewards," I said to both of them. "Being an investigator means making sacrifices."

We finished up and I teetered across the street to an army surplus store, my associates, even hefty Kitty, outpacing me. Cora Mae's teensy boots were killing my feet.

Glass cases framed the service desk and held the goodies we needed. A young boy with a large red pimple on the end of his nose and a mouth full of metal braces stood at the case.

"I'd like to look at those handcuffs," Cora Mae said to him, pointing.

"What do we need handcuffs for?" I said.

"I'm just looking. Can't I look?" Cora Mae ran her fingers along the handcuffs like she was stroking a man's hairy chest. "I didn't know you could buy handcuffs."

"We'll take three pepper sprays," I said to the clerk, "and where are your stun guns? Cora Mae, you need a stun gun. You, too, Kitty."

"Don't carry stun guns," the clerk said.

"Why not?"

"Illegal."

"Oh," I said, clutching my stun gun-loaded purse tight against my body. "Three of those whistles on a rope."

He rang our order up and put our purchases in a bag.

"You can throw these in, too," Cora Mae said, handing him the handcuffs. "Never know when you'll need a pair."

———

On the way out of town, I spotted a sporting goods store and we stopped in for ammo. I bought more buckshot and a few slugs, then spotted a fly-fishing vest with all kinds of little pockets, and bought that, too.

When we got back to the truck, I took off Cora Mae's plaid coat and put on the vest. Then I filled the pockets with ammo and the pepper spray, and put the rope with the whistle around my neck. With Cora Mae's coat back on, you couldn't tell that I was a walking arsenal.

———

I dropped Cora Mae at her house, but couldn't get rid of Kitty. She stuck like a spider on duct tape.

"How can I protect you if I'm not with you," she reasoned.

I had to figure out a way to ditch her soon.

We drove over to check out the damage to my home. Blaze's sheriff's truck was parked in my driveway. I parked behind his truck and walked around it.

Kitty whistled. "What happened to his truck?"

In the light of day the paint job didn't look as good as it had in the barn. That's the trouble with working without natural sunlight. I should have pulled the truck out into the sun instead of spraying it inside. I noticed that I had sprayed too much in some areas and the paint had dripped down the side of the truck. The rust spots were a deep yellow, the color of a pumpkin just starting to ripen, while the rest of the truck was canary yellow.

The whole thing reminded me of an overused paint rag. I wasn't about to mention it to Blaze in case he hadn't noticed. He isn't very observant. Maybe a darker yellow paint would fix it right. When I found time away from my investigation work, I'd have to work on it.

Once this court stuff was dropped.

The damage inside my house looked worse in the light of day, too. I stood in the doorway wondering how it could ever be cleaned up when Blaze came around from the back of the house.

Looking pale and tired, he said, "I've installed new deadbolts." He handed me a set of keys. "You'll have to fill out an insurance claim, and Little Donny and Mary offered to help you clean up."

The only good thing I could see in having my house vandalized was it gave Blaze something to do. It would keep him out of my way, off chasing burglars while I investigated Chester's murder.

I packed enough clothes for an extended slumber party at Cora Mae's. I noticed Chester's smut magazines on the top shelf of the hall closet and stuffed them into my suitcase. Tonight's entertainment.

"Keep Little Donny a few more nights," I said to Blaze. "I'm not ready to move back in yet. Besides, I like sleepovers."

Blaze carried my suitcase out to the truck, looking down at the ground while he walked and not saying anything. He opened the door and helped me up, loaded the suitcase in the passenger seat, heaved Kitty up, then stood and watched me try to back down the driveway straight. I didn't look back as I drove away.

———

Cora Mae isn't much of a cook. The blueberry pancakes she'd made earlier this morning were store-bought frozen pancakes, not the real McCoy. I should have picked up food supplies at Ray's general store, but I forgot how she is.

We had skipped lunch so I was starving, and the lettuce salad she put in front of me didn't fill me up. The down side of staying with Cora Mae was going to be food. I made a mental note to whip up a few casseroles in my spare time.

When Kitty called her third cousin and he appeared in the driveway with a big serving bowl filled with beef stew, I could have hugged her, but I refrained. We aren't over-eager to show affection in Finn country, at least not publicly. No hugging, kissing, or hand holding in public: that's pretty much a standard rule.

After Cousin Jeff roared off, Kitty plunked into a kitchen chair and spread her legs. I tried not to look.

"Thought you might like some decent grub so I whipped this up earlier," she said, glancing at Cora Mae. "No offense, Cora Mae."

"None taken, dear," Cora Mae said as she warmed up the stew.

Kitty was still huffing from the exertion of climbing down the steps to meet Jeff and then mounting them again. I hope if I ever need Kitty to defend me that it doesn't involve physical movement on her part or I'm as good as dead.

Cora Mae set cups of coffee in front of us and sat down herself.

"Why isn't Bill living on some of his father's property?" I asked. "All that land, it stands to reason he'd live there."

"Bill and his old man never got along much," Kitty said, between bites. "Bill couldn't be the macho man Chester wanted him to be. Bill's little and skinny, and when he started doing office work for a living, Chester said it was a girl's job. They've always been at each other's throats. When he took up with the Southern blonde, Chester really went nuts."

"I can't picture Bill killing Chester," I said.

"Nah," Kitty said. "No way. Bill's against guns, you know. Won't have them around. Another reason his pa was ticked. Bill wouldn't even hunt."

"I wonder how we can find out if anyone had an insurance policy on Chester," I said.

"Ask Blaze," Cora Mae said. "Maybe he has some ideas."

Oh, right, Blaze would tell me.

Kitty stayed to watch the news on television, then rocked herself up from the couch with help from Cora Mae and stood several feet inside my comfort zone. I instinctively backed up. She followed me.

"Jeff's picking me up out front," she said. "You stay in tonight with Cora Mae. No investigating without your bodyguard."

After Kitty left, Cora Mae set her hair in big rollers and spread cream on her face while I unpacked my suitcase.

"Look what I found out at Chester's blind," I said, holding up the magazines.

Cora Mae clapped her hands. "Sex magazines! I've always wanted to look at one of those."

We settled on the couch and each of us paged through a magazine. Every once in a while Cora Mae would giggle and show me a picture she thought was special. We weren't interested in the women, but the men were butt-naked, too.

Suddenly Cora Mae screamed in my ear.

"Ouch," I said, holding my ear. "That really hurt."

"Cripes," she said. "Look at this."

She shoved the magazine in front of my face, too close to see. I took it from her and held it out. There, in all her glory, was Barb Lampi. Two full pages had been devoted to her. The staples binding the magazine together sliced through her belly button. She had the biggest boobs I've ever seen.

"Guess those weren't falsies after all," I said to Cora Mae, whose mouth was frozen open like the mounted trout at Herb's bar.

"Implants," she managed to mutter.

I searched the caption. "It says her name is Thelma Thompson."

"Maybe that's her stage name," Cora Mae said.

"I doubt she'd change her name from Barb to Thelma. It'd be the other way around. No, I think that's her real name, and I bet Barb is an alias."

Cora Mae stared at the page. "Chester must have found these magazines and confronted her. Then she snuck out to the blind and killed him."

"Women don't shoot people," I said, shaking my head. "They run them over with their cars or poison them. When's the last time you heard of a woman murdering a man with a rifle?"

Cora Mae shrugged. "Maybe she hired someone."

We paged through the rest of the magazines and found her in each one, although she received top billing only in the first one.

It was time for a little talk with Barb.

"It's time for a little dint," I said.

"Dint?"

"Dint."

EIGHT

Word for the Day
INCURSION (in KUR zhuhn) n.
A sudden, brief invasion or raid.

BRIGHT AND EARLY TUESDAY morning while we were enjoying our coffee and cinnamon rolls, Blaze pulled into Cora Mae's driveway in his yellow sheriff's truck.

I watched him from the kitchen window as he lumbered to the door and pounded on the frame.

"My, my," Cora Mae said when she opened the door and noticed his truck, "what happened to your truck?"

"Got near a lunatic," he said, nodding at me.

"You'll regret calling me names once I'm dead and gone. You'll regret a lot of things when I'm gone. But back to business. How are you progressing with the break-in?"

Blaze was more grim-faced than usual this morning. "That's what I want to talk to you about." He sat down at the table with his winter jacket still on and wrapped his big paws around the cup of coffee Cora Mae set in front of him. "Do you want to do this in private?" He glanced over at Cora Mae.

"I don't have any secrets from my friends."

"What I believe happened, Ma," he said, taking my hand in his and answering slowly, "is that you vandalized your own home."

"What?" I screamed. "Have you completely lost your mind?"

Blaze had his arm out stiff like he was stopping traffic. "I'm trying to understand. I really am. But you have to talk to me. Maybe you don't want to live alone anymore and it's your way of reaching out."

I wanted to reach out all right and clutch Blaze by his cologne-drenched throat.

Cora Mae popped up and grabbed the coffee pot. "More coffee?"

I had my hands on the back of one of the kitchen chairs, squeezing hard. Blaze hadn't even been looking for the person who destroyed my home. Was he completely dense?

"Convince me then," Blaze said. "Give me a good alibi. Little Donny and George were at your house right before the card game. Right?"

"That's right. They can vouch for me." I couldn't believe I had to defend myself against my own son. Again.

"But you didn't come over for the game with them. In fact, we waited so long, at one point we thought you weren't coming at all."

I narrowed my eyes. "What are you implying? That I used the time to vandalize my own house?" When Blaze gave me a steady stare, I slammed my hand down on the table.

Blaze leaned forward and said, "I want you to pack up and move over with Mary and me until we sort this out. Until your place is cleaned up."

"No thanks," I said through a clenched jaw. "Think I'll pass. As far as I'm concerned, it's already sorted out."

"I'm not giving you a choice, Ma. I'm going to stay right here until you're packed and then I'm following you over to the house." Blaze gave Cora Mae, who was listening for once instead of gabbing, a weak smile.

"Cora Mae," I said. "I'm staying right here."

"Of course, you are," she said clearing her throat. "Maybe you two can reach a compromise. I hate to see you fighting. You're family."

"You're better off without one," I told Cora Mae.

"I have my date with Onni tonight," she said, slowly. "And since I'm cooking for him here, and . . ."

"Okay, okay," I said, her message coming through loud and clear. I didn't intend to be the third wheel in what was obviously going to be a love-in. "How about I come over and spend the night," I said to Blaze, concentrating on slowing my breathing. "But only one night. We can have a nice talk."

"It's a start," he said, sounding relieved. Was it possible that Blaze believed all the stuff he made up?

Besides, I reasoned with myself, I can't give up Mary and Little Donny just because Blaze is acting like a jerk, and I'd have another chance to talk Blaze out of court. If I changed my mind before this evening, I could always stay at my house in spite of the mess.

"You didn't tell him about the magazines," Cora Mae whispered when he went into the living room to make a phone call.

"It's like playing poker, Cora Mae. You put one card down at a time."

———

"Blaze thinks I destroyed my own house for attention," I said to Kitty, who had appeared before we could make a get-away.

"And—"

"And what? I didn't do it. Do you realize how outrageous that is? Think about it."

"Who knew you weren't home?"

"My truck was parked right out front because I walked over, so whoever did it might not have known I wasn't home." That thought sent shivers down my spine. "The only people who knew I wasn't home were the guys at the card table—Blaze, Little Donny, and George." A thought struck me. "You don't suppose Blaze had my house vandalized to make me look bad for our court appearance?"

"No one's that low," Kitty said. "Not even Blaze."

———

Kitty's yard looked like the town dump. The neighbors had been trying to make her clean it up for years without any luck. They'd even had a meeting at the town hall and sent an official letter ordering her to clean it up. Nothing so far.

She lived on a side road right off of Highway 35, so everyone going into and out of town got to sightsee past Kitty's. It was the perfect place for a rummage sale. The beauty of it was maybe someone might haul off some of her garbage along with the actual rummage items.

"What did you bring?" Kitty said as we unloaded boxes from the back of the truck and added them to the junk heap.

"This and that," I said. "Some of the boxes are filled with Barney's things, books mainly. I didn't look through them. You can do that."

"Gertie, you should keep them if they were Barney's."

"I haven't needed any of this in the last fourteen months, and I won't need any of it now." Barney was an avid reader and would reread the same books. I'm more of a one-time reader. There are so many good books waiting to be read, I'll never go back and read one twice.

I spotted a notebook lying in the pile and picked it up. I smiled. It was Barney's writing notebook. "Think I'll keep this, though."

"See," Cora Mae said. "We better go through the boxes and make sure you really want to get rid of the things in them."

"You do it. I don't want to."

Cora Mae and Kitty lugged the boxes into Kitty's living room, which was an extension of her junky yard, and sat on the floor and began sorting. I settled into a recliner and paged through Barney's notebook. Every once in a while, Cora Mae held something up for my examination and each time I said the same thing, "Sell it."

Halfway through the notebook entries I turned a page and a loose paper slid to the floor. Kitty handed it back.

I couldn't believe what I held in my hand. I shot up straight in the recliner.

In my hand I held the mineral rights to Chester Lampi's property, and the owner, the name appearing at the bottom of the document, was my deceased husband, Barney. He'd signed it and had it notarized.

"I think I know why someone vandalized my house," I said, showing the paper to the rest of my investigative team. "They were looking for this."

"Why didn't you tell us you owned the rights?" Cora Mae said, not quite behind the eight ball as usual.

"I didn't know until just this minute. Why would Barney have the mineral rights and keep it from me?"

"Maybe he didn't think it was important," Kitty suggested. "Maybe he forgot. And if this was what the burglar was looking for, why didn't he find it?"

"Because I had already boxed the notebook up along with the other things for the rummage sale and put them in the shed. The shed wasn't touched." I read the fine print one more time. "We checked at the Register of Deeds and according to their records, Onni owns the mineral rights. This is getting messier by the minute."

Kitty struggled up from the floor. "If I remember right, the deed we looked at in Escanaba showed Onni's ownership going back a good fifty years. The date on this document is two years ago. Onni must have transferred the rights and Barney never filed the new ownership papers."

I thought hard. "If Chester died because of the land and if the mineral rights had anything to do with it, the logical suspect is a family member. Do you think Barb searched my house?"

"A lot of what-ifs going on here," Kitty added.

"If Barb searched your house," Cora Mae said, "she would have taken the magazines."

"What magazines?" Kitty demanded. "What's going on? If I'm going to protect you properly, you have to keep me informed."

"You'd think," I said, ignoring Kitty and waving the document in the air, "this piece of paper's as valuable as gold."

———

The snow started falling in the early afternoon, not slow and lazy, but thick so it stuck to my eyelashes and wet my face. I ran for the truck at the first opportunity, surprise etched on Cora Mae's and Kitty's faces. Kitty gave chase but I pulled away from her on the front porch. What a surprise that Kitty couldn't hold her own in a footrace.

I hated deceiving Cora Mae, but I needed a break from Kitty's overbearing bodyguard strategies, and it was the only way I could think of to get away.

Kitty stomped her foot and blasted away on the whistle she wore on a rope around her neck, the same one we had bought in Escanaba. A steady scream from the whistle assaulted my poor ears until I pulled away. I made a mental note never to buy Kitty another present as I rounded the corner and breathed in the sweet smell of freedom.

After finding no one home at Blaze's, I parked in my own drive. Pulling my shotgun from under the seat, I trudged through the gathering snow to my hunting blind.

I was tired. Up until last Tuesday the most excitement I had to look forward to was the afternoon paper's crossword puzzle or bingo at the Indian casino. All that's changed. Chester's murdered, I'm driving for the first time in my life, and an intruder searched my home. Pretty exciting stuff, but I was tuckered out. And the mineral rights that Barney owned, and that I now owned, had me baffled.

Who cared about the mineral rights? What good were they? Copper country was north of us. Whoever wanted the document, wanted it bad. Part of me wanted to run right over to Escanaba and file it, another part wanted more time to think. I stuffed the paper into the cushion of the La-Z-Boy before I sat down.

Starting the heater, I kicked back for an afternoon snooze, feeling my problems drifting away.

The afternoon light was fading when I woke up, and the snow still fell, blowing against the blind. A doe and her half-grown fawn grazed on the apple pile.

I waded through a foot of snow, wiped off the windshield of my truck with a plastic scraper, and headed to Blaze's for supper.

———

The mobile home smelled like wet socks. Little Donny was lying on an afghan-covered couch with his feet propped up on the armrest.

"Get yourself up and change those socks before the fumes kill us all," I said, swatting him gently on the head. "Move it."

Little Donny lumbered down the narrow hall. I looked around. Everything was neat as a pin. Each piece of furniture was covered with squares of wool in every imaginable color, left over from Mary's afghan craze. She sure was a whiz with crochet needles. Mary spent way too much time on housework and handiwork instead of working on interesting things.

Blaze looked up from the *Tamarack Reporter* he was reading. "Saw your truck parked at the house and looked around for you. Figured you were hunting at the blind. See anything?"

"Not a thing," I said, remembering my nap.

Ten minutes later we sat down to fried chicken, canned creamed corn, and mashed potatoes.

Mary smiled when she told me I could sleep in the sewing room. "The couch pulls out into a bed. It's already made up."

Little Donny would stay in the living room where he'd slept last night.

"Maybe we can have a talk about this court thing tomorrow morning. I won't be around much tonight," I said, spooning creamed corn onto my potatoes. "I'm working on a case."

"No, Ma," Blaze said in a controlled voice. "I'm working on a case. Remember, I'm the sheriff. That's my job."

"Yes, I know, but I'm assisting."

"No, you're not. You're going to hunt deer out in your blind a little and take nice naps in the afternoons, and keep out of my business. It's time to retire."

I didn't say anything, just went on eating. I never listened to Blaze my whole life and wasn't about to start now.

I remembered I needed to use my word for the day and rummaged in my pockets for the scrap of paper. It wasn't there. This word-a-day idea sounded good at the beginning but was quickly becoming a chore. I couldn't remember yesterday's word or the day before's word. I couldn't even remember today's word without a cheat-sheet, and now I'd lost it.

"And just to keep you safe and honest," Blaze said, interrupting my thoughts. "I'm assigning you your own private bodyguard."

I smiled. "I already have a bodyguard."

"And who would that be?"

"Kitty's taking care of me."

"Kitty couldn't protect a three-legged dog. Little Donny's going to keep an eye on you. Day and night, he's going to know right where you are. Isn't that right, Little Donny?"

"Geez," Little Donny whined. "Do I have to?"

Blaze glared at him. Little Donny looked away first. I thought this was a fine arrangement. The thought of Little Donny hanging around was appealing. He would be easy to lose if I wanted him lost, and he might even be helpful. I wish I'd thought of it first. Kitty could share the job with Little Donny, a great excuse when I needed time away from her.

"Little Donny," I said, "I think it's a wonderful idea."

Poor Donny laid his head in his hands, defeated.

After supper clean-up, Blaze and Mary went to visit Grandma Johnson with a plate of chicken, and Little Donny, my new personal bodyguard, fell asleep on the couch.

Snow was still coming down thick and heavy when I started the truck and pulled out. I waited until I drove out onto the main road before I put on the lights.

I noticed after the first mile that I'd picked up a tail. By the second mile I figured out who it was. I pulled over, rolled down the window and motioned the trailing car over to the side of my truck. The car crept up on the left side and stopped, the window sliding down. "Might as well make yourself useful," I said to Kitty.

———

Kitty wasn't dressed for outdoor work, which served her right for following me around. I hoped she'd suffer, but I hadn't anticipated the amount of junk that woman carried around in her car. She rummaged in the trunk and came back to the truck carrying a load of clothes.

"Hop in," I said. "We'll pick up your car later."

She grinned like she'd been invited to my private party, instead of the truth, which was that she'd crashed it.

I wore my fishing vest under my hunting jacket and it was fully loaded. I had pepper spray, ammo, hand and foot warmers, and a thermos of Tang. The stun gun was tucked in my purse, and my shotgun lay on the cab floor. I had dressed for subzero weather because this was a surveillance run, and we were going to be outside.

Kitty fussed and complained as she struggled into long underwear and an old army fatigue jacket.

"If you want to run surveillance," I said, watching her attempt to button the jacket, which turned out to belong to her cousin and was several sizes too small, "you have to be prepared."

After driving by Bill and Barb's house several times, we parked down the road. I could see light filtering through drawn drapes. With the garage door down, we didn't know if they were home or not. Lights on didn't mean much. Some people don't bother turning them off, especially if they're only going to be gone a short while.

"Let's sneak around back and take a peek inside a window," I said, dropping down from the truck. The weight of my weapons vest almost bowled me over face first. "Watch that first step, Kitty. It's a killer."

I burst out laughing when I glanced over at her.

"Shhh," she hissed. "Don't let everyone know we're coming."

She had on a black facemask to keep her face warm, and she looked like she was ready to rob the Escanaba bank. She was wrapped in so many layers of clothing she could have passed for King Kong. Snow settled on her head as we crouched in the shadows.

We probably should have talked about a plan, but I had a general idea. If they weren't home, we would let ourselves in and do a quick search, looking mostly for incriminating evidence like big insurance policies or airline tickets for Tahiti or documents referring to Chester's land. If they were home, the best we could do was watch for suspicious behavior.

They were home. We could see them through the kitchen window, sitting at the table with a bottle of beer in front of each of them and a stack of papers between them.

Settling in the shadow twenty feet from the window, I rummaged in my vest and hauled out a pair of binoculars. I tried to get a better look at the papers on the table, but the binoculars steamed over every time I put them up to my face. When a thin crust of ice formed on the lenses I gave up, put them back in my pocket, and edged closer.

Fifteen minutes later they still sat there talking.

"Can you read lips?" I whispered to Kitty.

She shook her head.

If they had looked out the window, they wouldn't have seen us we were so piled with snow. Kitty shook from the cold, her teeth rattling.

We were on our way back to the truck, rounding the house on the side, when we heard knocking at the front door. Stopping and peering in a dining room window, I saw Bill move through the house. The window gave us a perfect view of the front door when Bill opened it.

Little Donny stood on the porch.

"Can I talk to my granny?" we heard Little Donny say. He craned his neck to look around Bill.

"What makes you think she's here?" Bill wanted to know.

Barb walked right by the window we were watching through and stopped behind Bill. I could almost have reached around the corner of the house and tugged on Little Donny's jacket, we were that close to him.

"Her truck's parked on the road out front." Little Donny turned and pointed off into the dark toward the road. "I'm supposed to be watching her and she gave me the slip. Blaze'll skin me alive if I don't find her fast. Isn't she here?"

Kitty and I were creeping down the side of the drive trying to stay out of the porch light when Kitty stopped abruptly and I plowed into the back of her. I steadied myself and looked back at the tracks following us away from the corner of the house. It better keep snowing, I thought, or in the morning they'll see our prints all around the back of the house.

"I have an idea," Kitty whispered. "Come on."

And she clomped right out onto the driveway and headed for the house calling out, "Hey, everybody, sure are glad you're home. Hey, Little Donny, what are you doing here?"

Kitty should have pulled off the black facemask. Not looking as if she was about to rob them blind would have lent credibility to whatever lie she was about to concoct. Little Donny took a step back toward the inside of the house, His eyes wide and round like coffee saucers, but he relaxed once he saw me coming up behind.

"Granny," he said in relief, "where have you been?" He kept an eye on Kitty, who still hadn't figured out she better unmask. I decided to step in since the woman with the brilliant idea was keeping it to herself.

"We're freezing," I said to Bill. "If you let us come inside and thaw out, maybe we can talk Kitty into taking off her face mask. Our truck broke down out on the road and we almost froze to death working on it. Little Donny, you run down and check it out. There are battery cables in the back. Maybe you can get it started."

"Why didn't I see you when I passed the truck?" he asked, puzzled. "I stopped and checked inside."

Kitty and I looked at each other. "We walked back the other way some," Kitty said. "You must have passed us in the dark."

I handed the truck keys to him and watched him pull out, driving Blaze's sheriff's truck.

Bill swung the door open. "Better come out of the snow."

We were in.

————

"I have to go to the bathroom," I said, melting snow pooling on the floor around my feet. I removed my boots, but remembered just in time to keep my hunting jacket on. It wouldn't be smart to expose my weapon vest. Bill pointed down the hall and I went, trailing clumps of snow falling from my clothes.

I searched through the medicine cabinet first, finding the usual things plus a couple of prescription drugs—Valium and an antibiotic. The cabinet under the sink held the usual—toilet paper, and a small trash can. The counter was covered with cosmetics, and an ashtray overflowed with stubs of menthol cigarettes.

Finishing my search, I opened my vest and extracted the thermos, pouring the Tang down the sink to relieve some of the weight. I had started to feel like I had concrete tied around my waist. I still looked like a beached whale with all my supplies.

When I came out of the bathroom I found Kitty sitting on a flowered sofa drinking out of a mug. Her jacket and facemask lay in a pile by the door, and she looked comfy as if she was nesting. Bill sat across from her.

While Kitty told him about the truck breakdown, a pretty believable story, I wandered around the room with my hands behind my back, scanning for clues. I studied family pictures on the top of the television. There was one of Chester when he still had his hair, with his arm around a young Bill. Bill had changed over the years too, but even back then he wore thick glasses.

"How you doing since your dad died?" I said to Bill, interrupting Kitty's work of fiction.

"Dad and I had a falling out in the last few years," Bill said sadly, shaking his head. "He got ornerier as he aged, and we disagreed on so much. I wish I'd had a chance to make up with him before he died."

"I'm sure he knew how you felt, deep down."

"I have more pictures. Do you want to see them?"

"Sure," I said, watching him take an album from the mantle. Just my luck. Trapped looking at photo albums. I plunked down next to Kitty in all my gear and paged through the album Bill handed to us.

I started sweating because of the heavy clothes I wore. It was only a matter of time before I passed out from the heat. Pulling off my hunting cap, I shook out my orange mop. I rolled up the legs of my snow pants. That was a trick, leaning down over all the supplies.

"Where's Barb?" I asked.

"She went to bed," Bill said.

"I need a drink of water." I handed the album to Kitty.

"You stay here," I said to Bill when he started to rise. "I can get it myself."

I opened every cupboard and drawer, again finding only the usual supplies. The pile of papers on the table turned out to be shopping catalogs.

Noticing the silence in the front room, I ran water in the sink and clinked a glass against the tap.

I was really on fire now, sweat beading on my forehead.

Just then Little Donny pounded on the front door and let himself in. When I turned off the water and came out of the kitchen he was blowing on his hands to warm them.

"Where are your gloves?" I asked. I motioned to Kitty with my head to get going and leaned against the wall to pull on my boots.

"Forgot them," Little Donny said. "There wasn't a thing wrong with your truck. It started right up."

"Well, that's certainly strange," I said, trying to hustle them out.

"Look at this one, Gertie." Kitty held up an aging black and white photograph of three servicemen, their arms around each other, smiles on their faces. "Chester and Onni and, why, isn't that Floyd?"

Bill looked over Kitty's shoulder. "The three of them enlisted in the Marines together. They were close friends their entire lives."

I studied the picture, trying to imagine bible-toting Floyd in the military, and even in his youth, Onni had the body of a scarecrow, a receding hairline, and a shifty, shaded light in his eyes like he was always prowling. I penciled him in on my mental suspect list.

It took a while to get Kitty moving, but finally we were on our way down the driveway, waving to Bill, who stood in the doorway watching us leave.

"That went well," I said to Kitty as we headed back to drop her off. "I don't think they suspect a thing."

NINE

Word for the Day
EGREGIOUS (ee GREE juhs) adj.
Outstanding for undesirable qualities;
remarkably bad; flagrant.

THE NEXT MORNING, I stayed in bed longer than usual, even though I was wide-awake. Blaze and Mary's sleeper sofa was comfy and warm. It felt good to stretch and wiggle my toes and think about the case. I could hear Little Donny's steady sawing from the living room as events marched through my head like wasps in and out of a hive.

I was learning a lot about being a detective, but I knew I had so much more to learn. There's nothing like the actual experience to teach you the finer points. Like what happened last night. It wasn't Little Donny's fault our cover was almost blown—I take full responsibility for it. Next time I go on a surveillance mission, I won't leave my truck smack dab in the road for everyone to see. All my life I've had to learn things the hard way.

The photograph of the three servicemen intrigued me: Chester—dead, a bullet in his head, owner of a large parcel of property, and Onni—one-time owner of the mineral rights for said piece of property, and in my book, an undesirable. As Grandma Johnson would say, from the muddy side of the pasture. Then we have Floyd, the bible belter who found Chester's body in the hunting shack. The fading photograph reminded me that life was precious and too short and that I should make every minute count.

By the time I arrived in the kitchen ready for the day, Blaze and Mary were nowhere in sight. I made a fresh pot of coffee and ate a doughnut, careful not to wake my personal bodyguard.

———

I poked around in my barn for things to add to Kitty's rummage pile, and a few minutes later, George pulled in. His snake-trimmed hat grinned at me and so did he.

"Get rid of that stray dog yet?" George asked. I noticed he had put on a brown wool sweater. The weather had been unseasonably cold, even for the U.P., and I wondered if George would hold out until January without a jacket.

"What stray dog?" I said, trying to wrestle an old bike out of a tangled heap.

"You know, the one with the yellow eyes." George pitched in and the bike came loose, the tires flat, rust corroding the handlebars.

"George, you sure are starting to drink early in the day. Better watch that. It'll ruin you."

George leaned his shoulder against a support beam. "Thought so," he said under his breath.

Then I remembered about the stun gun and the fib I'd told George. "Oh, he's around here all right but he hasn't got near enough to zap."

An amused grin spread over his face as he looked at my pile and the bike. "What are you doing with that?"

"Kitty's having a rummage sale," I said. "I thought I'd donate some of the family's old things. She could use the money. Make sure you stop and buy something. This though . . ." I gestured at the bike, "should go to the dump."

George nodded. "I'll drop it off. The reason I came by was to remind you about tonight. The Lion's Club is having its annual pastie dinner and dance. The Lionesses are doin' the cooking."

"That's right. I forgot all about it."

"Thought I could escort you over there."

My mind was working a mile a minute. Everybody in the county goes to the pastie dinner, which meant Bill and Barb would be there, which meant an empty Lampi house and the possibility of tying up a few loose ends. Although this case had more than a few ends flying loose.

"That would be nice," I said, "only you go on ahead and have fun. I'll meet you there. Cora Mae and I have something to do first. It'll make us a little late."

"Sure, fine by me. How about a game of cards this afternoon."

"I have to go to court," I said. "Today's the day."

George shuffled his feet and, if I didn't know better, I would have thought the expression flickering across his handsome face resembled disappointment.

I dug an empty cardboard box out of the corner and began to fill it. George helped me load the boxes for Kitty's rummage sale into the bed of my truck. Then he loaded a pile of things for the dump into the back of his truck. What a man, I thought, watching him close the back end up, stroll to the driver's seat with a tip of his hat, and drive off.

I pulled a drill and a box of wood screws off of the tool cart and headed back to Blaze's.

The night before when I got ready for bed, I noticed that some of the floorboards in Blaze's mobile home were squeaky, especially in the hall. Living in a small trailer and listening to creaks and groans from loose boards could drive anyone absolutely crazy, a theory I'll have to explore regarding Blaze's recent behavior. He must be too busy trying to get out of work to notice when his own home needs repair. He never was handy with tools.

Never wait for a man to do a job that's important to you, is my motto, because the job will never get done. Or he'll mess it up something awful and you'll have to either fix it yourself anyway or learn to live with it the way it is. A woman can do anything if she has the proper tools. And Barney had left a barn full for me.

I plugged the drill into a hall electrical socket and began drilling the screws into the floor using the screw attachment. I ended up using the whole box. It was a good thing the floor was bare wood instead of linoleum or tile. That would have been harder.

Little Donny came out of the bathroom in his boxers and a white undershirt, toweling his damp hair. He squeezed down the hall past me, shaking his head. Mornings are especially rough on him.

My repair job ended up looking pretty good, and when I tested it the floor was as quiet as one of Grandma Johnson's cooked noodles.

———

"What the hell happened to my maple floor," Blaze hollered when he came home a little later. "Mary, come and see what she did now. Oh, my God."

He clamped his hands on the sides of his face and squeezed like he had a migraine headache.

"It doesn't look a bit worse than it did before," I said. "And it's quieter like it should be, and Mary's not home yet. She's visiting with Grandma."

Blaze had one hand over his mouth, and he was that red tomato color again. It figures that Blaze wouldn't appreciate what I did for him. He's always been that way, but I'm not a quitter. I'll keep it up till one day he says thank you and means it.

"Maybe you have too many clothes on," I said to him, remembering how I'd overheated at Bill's because I had on so much. "Dress lighter and maybe that red coloring will go away. Wouldn't hurt to try. And once it gets walked on a bit," I added, "the shine on those screws will wear away."

———

"The bullet that killed Chester was from his own weapon," Kitty said while riding shotgun with Cora Mae scrunched in the middle. "He was killed with a rifle from the gun rack at his house."

135

"How do you know that?" I said, excited and almost drove the truck into the ditch. I pulled over and slammed on the brakes. "Who told you?"

"I have sources in Escanaba," Kitty said, smugly.

"Does Blaze know about this?"

Kitty nodded. "He must. He'd get the report as soon as it was ready."

"You'd think I'd be the first one he'd share it with since I was the first one with the murder theory. Figures he'd know and not even tell me. The killer made a mistake putting the murder weapon back," I reasoned. "If he had dumped the rifle, nobody ever would have known it was Chester's own rifle."

"If you hadn't noticed the extra rifle in the gun rack Blaze never would have had it checked," Kitty said. "You're a hero."

I was starting to like Kitty more and more all the time. "I thought he ignored pretty much everything I said. I'm expecting a full apology from him. A public one." Frowning, I decided it didn't make sense. If I planned out a murder, would I use my victim's rifle? "Why would a killer use the victim's own weapon to murder him?"

"Smart, I think," Kitty said. "Impossible to trace to the killer. All evidence would point back to the victim."

"Get back on the road," Cora Mae said to me, "or you'll be late for court. And didn't I say to dress up nice? You're just asking to lose your case."

I pulled back onto the road.

"What's wrong with the way I'm dressed?" I could feel Cora Mae and Kitty making faces at each other. I wore a brown work jacket over black pants and a green sweatshirt. I had on my hunting boots since the forecast called for more snow.

Cora Mae was dressed like she was going to hang around the downtown lamppost. She had on purple high heels and a fluffy, quilted red coat that barely fit in the truck considering the space reserved for Kitty's bulk. At least she wasn't wearing her funeral black.

Kitty wore some kind of tent thing over her housedress and hadn't bothered to take out her pin curls. Apparently, in her mind, a court appearance didn't warrant a comb-out.

"What's going to happen in court today?" Cora Mae asked.

"They're going to dismiss the case," I said. "Blaze doesn't have a case. He's probably waiting for me to arrive so he can apologize for doubting me. Then he'll change his mind about taking me to court."

We approached Escanaba, driving along the shore of Lake Michigan, waves pounding onto the rocks, seagulls cruising the wind overhead.

"Don't you want to know about my date with Onni?" Cora Mae cooed.

"Every last detail," Kitty said.

"Only the part about the land," I said quickly before Cora Mae could start in on more details than I'd ever want to know.

"Here's what happened in a nutshell. Way back when, years ago, Chester's dad won the land from Onni's dad in a poker game."

"Over three hundred acres lost in a card game." Kitty squealed. "And we play for pennies and match sticks. Imagine that."

"But Chester's family didn't win the mineral rights because Onni's dad wouldn't bet them away. No one knew why, although

Onni said there was a rumor going around that traces of gold were discovered back by Bear Creek and if it turned out someday to be true, owning the mineral rights would be important."

"Gold," I straightened up at that. "Gold in the U.P.?"

Kitty leaned over Cora Mae. "Haven't you ever heard of Old Ropes Gold Mine over by Ishpeming? That underground mine produced gold for fourteen years. Some folks think Tamarack County is the next hotbed."

"This is the dumbest thing I've ever heard," I said. "If someone had discovered gold, all of Stonely would be hunting for gold instead of hunting for Big Buck."

"Keep your eyes on the road," Cora Mae said to me in a loud voice as the right tire hit the gravel on the side of the road. I corrected quickly.

Kitty shook her head and the vibration traveled through Cora Mae and rippled against my side. "Rumor has it some people around here are making their living from secret locations of gold."

"Who? And where?" I wanted to know. "Who do we know? Everyone around here is poor as a wet-rot potato patch. If your theory is right, they must all be hiding their wealth behind broken-down houses. Besides, if that was true, Onni never would have turned the rights over to Barney."

"That's right," Cora Mae said. "Onni didn't believe it either."

"Why did he give it to Barney in the first place?" I pulled into the courthouse parking lot and crawled along scanning for an empty slot.

"He traded it for that old Ford tractor you used to have."

"Not the one he had to tow off because it had two flat tires and wouldn't start?"

"That's the one."

"Dumbest thing I've ever heard."

———

The Escanaba courthouse is imposing, impersonal, and the last place on earth I wanted to be at the moment. Our footsteps sounded like thunder, our whispers echoed ahead of us, heavy doors cracked close in the distance, and people with suspicion and pain in their eyes sat on uncomfortable benches, waiting and worrying and watching.

"The ugliest people in the world are in this courthouse," Kitty said, the harsh florescent lights turning her teeth an unhealthy yellow and enlarging her pores. "Gives me the creeps."

We sat outside the courtroom, stuffed together on a bench until Blaze arrived, surrounded by a group of people. They stood across the hall, heads together, and my hopes of a peaceful resolution dissipated like fog at dawn.

Blaze and I entered the courtroom like complete strangers, without acknowledging each other and without eye contact. Our entourages followed: Cora Mae and Kitty pressed tightly together like Siamese twins, and Blaze's two attorneys. Apparently one was not enough. He needed two devious legal minds to help him beat down and assure the complete defeat of one helpless woman.

A hearing was concluding so we slid onto more hard benches, Blaze and counsel on one side, Cora Mae, Kitty, and myself on the other.

An older woman, who I guessed to be around eighty-five years old, rose from a table at the front of the courtroom and confronted the opposing side, a quiver in her lips, moisture gleaming in her eyes.

"You can't keep me from going back to my home," she said, angrily. "You can't stop me."

I studied the two women she addressed with her comments. They had many of the woman's same features, her daughters I presumed. The attorney seated next to them, wearing a gray suit, smirked like she'd just crushed her opponent.

"How can you think this is funny?" the old woman said to the attorney.

I wondered what she could have possibly done to deserve this kind of treatment from her daughters. I wondered what I had done to deserve it from Blaze. I couldn't see his side of the picture at all.

The old woman's attorney hustled her out of the courtroom before she could cause a scene, and we moved up to the two tables in front of the judge's bench. The plan was for me to sit alone at one of the tables, and for Cora Mae and Kitty to sit right behind me. At the last moment as my name was announced, Kitty plunked down in the seat next to me at the table.

The judge, a little bitty man buried in an enormous robe, wore his hair in a military-style cropped cut and looked about twelve years old.

"This is a preliminary hearing to determine whether the case will be contested and to set a court date if necessary. Are you Mrs. Johnson's attorney?"

He looked at Kitty's pin-curled head.

"Yes, your honor," Kitty said, like she spent every day fighting courtroom crime.

Blaze whispered to his attorney, who then jumped up and informed the court that Kitty couldn't represent me.

"That's fine," I said into the microphone on the table. "I don't need to hire an attorney to tell you I'm not insane. I can tell you myself."

"Are you contesting the hearing?" the judge said to me, his expression unreadable.

"Absolutely."

"Then we will set a court date, and I advise you, Mrs. Johnson, to consult with an attorney. This is a serious issue, one an attorney can advise you best on."

One of Blaze's legal schmegals rose. "Your Honor, we are asking the court to set a date as soon as possible since there is some immediacy."

"The calendar is very full." The judge shuffled papers.

"Your Honor, Mrs. Johnson appears to be in need of immediate supervision. She has squandered her life savings, damaged the plaintiff's home and vehicle, and has allegedly vandalized her own home. In view of the new facts surrounding this case, we would like to request placement as well."

I looked at Kitty.

"That means," Kitty whispered, "they want to decide where you will live. They want to put you away in a nursing home."

I began to feel faint, a hot flush creeping up from the pit of my soul and scorching my face. If I slapped myself, maybe I'd wake up. "This is a gregarious act on my son's part." I shouted, leaping up.

Kitty leapt up also. "She means egregious, your honor."

I stared at her, remembering my word for the day, a remarkable feat considering the circumstances.

She smiled.

"We insist on speed," the other side demanded.

"Very well," the judge said. "We'll put it on the calendar for three weeks from now. That'll give Mrs. Johnson time to retain counsel, and I'm also ordering a psychological evaluation for Mrs. Johnson."

"We want a jury trial," Kitty shouted.

"We demand a psychological evaluation for the plaintiff, too," I shouted.

———

Kitty had to drive me home. I was too upset to drive. "If I ever speak to him again, it'll be too soon. This is it, the last straw. He's totally disowned. Don't ever mention his name again."

"Now, now," Cora Mae clucked. "Blaze really believes in his own mind that you need his care. Try to look at it from his point of view."

"Whose side are you on? His?"

"No! But I don't think he's intentionally doing it to hurt you. And the placement thing doesn't necessarily mean he wants to put you in a nursing home. Maybe he wants you to live with him."

Wallowing in self-pity isn't my style, but I was settling in to do a fairly good job of it until I noticed Kitty was driving about a hundred and twenty miles an hour and had taken the last corner on two wheels.

"Kitty," I said, "slow it down."

"This is one kick-ass truck," Kitty exclaimed. "Bet I can bury the needle."

She glanced over and I could see fire in her eyes. Pin curls were popping and the flab hanging from her arms bounced with the truck as it tore up the road. Cora Mae clutched my arm.

"Kitty," I shouted. "Pull my truck over to the side of the road. *now.*"

"Okay, okay, just trying to take your mind off your troubles." And she slowed down to a few volts under the speed of electricity. "Where we going next?"

"We are dropping you off at your house."

"No way. I'm your bodyguard. You're stuck with me till this case is solved. We can hang out at my place and you can pick out the things you want to buy before the rummage sale starts."

We argued over her role in my life until she pulled into her junkyard. "I'm not leaving without you," she said.

"Out." I whipped the stun gun out of my purse.

Cora Mae's eyes bulged. "You had that thing in court?"

"Out," I said again, poking it in Kitty's direction. "You work for me and you take orders from me, and I don't need you anymore today. Go find clues. Work with Cora Mae. Between the two of you, you ought to come up with something on the case."

"I can't believe you had a stun gun in court," Cora Mae said.

"You, too." I poked threateningly at Cora Mae. "Out."

The two of them rolled out of the truck and as I drove out of the driveway I could see Kitty running for her car.

I parked the truck inside Blaze's barn, closed the doors, and spent the rest of the afternoon hiding out in my hunting blind.

TEN

Word for the Day
KERFUFFLE (kuhr FUF uhl) n.
Disorder; uproar; confusion

"What's he doing here?" Cora Mae whispered to me when Little Donny and I picked her up for the pastie dinner. She wore a short black skirt under her unbuttoned coat, a tight-knit sweater that made her look like a thirty-eight double D, and black fishnet stockings.

"Couldn't get rid of him," I whispered back. "He's sticking like toilet paper on a shoe. I was cleaning up inside my house and he appeared. He won't go away."

I managed to stay one step ahead of him, though. I had the driver's seat of my truck and I wasn't giving it up.

Little Donny had on his fancy loafer shoes with the little tassels, beige dress pants, a blue shirt, and a long wool overcoat. I wore black cords and a black sweater with fall leaves swirled on the

144

front that matched the color of my hair. I had styled it loose and curly. My feet were cold, as usual, so I decided to wear my boots. I didn't plan on dancing anyway.

"You're turning the wrong way," Little Donny informed me.

"We have a stop to make first," I said.

The house was dark but the yard light illuminated the front and side of the house. Remembering our last fiasco, I made one pass on the road, looking for a good place to hide the truck. There wasn't one. Banks of snow on both sides of the road made it impossible to pull off. I turned into Bill and Barb's recently plowed driveway and stopped to mull the situation over. If I left the truck in the driveway under the yard light, anyone driving by would see my truck.

I backed up for a running start, gunned the engine, and headed for the snow in the shadow on the far side of the drive. Little Donny clutched the dashboard with his mouth in a perfect O. Cora Mae, sitting between us, held onto my arm.

The truck settled into a snow bank next to the driveway and I turned off the ignition. Little Donny rubbed his head where it had hit the dash.

I hopped down, waded through the snow, and lifted a toolbox out of the back. "Let's go, Cora Mae. Not you," I added when Little Donny opened his door. "You stay here and guard the truck." Breaking and entering was okay for us, but I didn't want my grandson involved. Wasn't that a perfect example of competent thinking? The very thing Blaze accused me of lacking.

"Blaze is going to kill us," he called after me. "We're stuck good, you know." His voice trailed off.

We went around the back of the house. Cora Mae began complaining that her black boots were going to be ruined, but I steered her onto the same path Kitty and I had made going through the night before, and she quieted down.

"What did you bring the toolbox for?" She said, her voice coy and cooing.

"How else are we getting in?"

"Maybe we should try these first." Cora Mae held up a ring of keys and dangled them.

"Hot dog," I said. "Where did you get those?"

"I snitched them from Kitty. She took them from a hook by the door when you two were running your brilliant surveillance scheme." Cora Mae giggled. "When you ditched us today, she showed them to me and I lifted them."

"Way to go."

"I feel terrible about leaving her behind. You should be kinder to her, Gertie."

"All I needed was a little time away. She's pretty intense. I didn't know she was going to take the bodyguard job so seriously." I did feel a few pangs of guilt. "She's beginning to grow on me," I said. That comment surprised both of us, earning a quick doubletake from Cora Mae, but it was true. I missed her.

We let ourselves in, and Cora Mae put the keys on a hook by the door. I pulled two flashlights from my jacket and handed one to Cora Mae. "You search the closets, I'll do the drawers. And be careful. Put everything back right where it belongs. We don't want them to know we were here."

Within minutes I found a handgun in Barb's panty drawer. I wrapped a pair of undies around it to avoid fingerprints and held it up for Cora Mae to see, wondering out loud, "If Bill hates guns like I hear he does, do you think he knows about this?"

Fascinated with Barb's clothes, Cora Mae didn't answer. She held up a sheath dress. "I'd look good in this," she said.

"This isn't Kitty's rummage sale," I said, stuffing the gun into the drawer. "Put it back."

Cora Mae reluctantly hung the dress in the closet and followed me into a small bedroom used as an office. I scoped out the desk while Cora Mae worked through a three-drawer file cabinet.

Nothing.

"I'm looking through Bill's desk again," I said, rooting through his papers. I pulled out and examined each folder, then did the same with the file cabinet. There wasn't anything bearing Chester's name in the whole bunch, nothing about the land.

"My two chief suspects at the moment are Barb and Bill, with Onni running a distant third," I said, perplexed. "There has to be something here.

"Maybe Onni killed Chester because of the land," Cora Mae whispered. "Maybe I dated a killer."

"Killing Chester wouldn't get Onni's land back. With Chester gone, the land belongs to Bill. Onni doesn't have a motive."

"Whew. That's a relief. For a minute there I was worried."

"But he could have killed Chester in a fit of rage that he'd lost the land. Whoever vandalized my home knew a lot about rage since he went beyond a normal search."

"Now I'm worried again."

Discouraged, I collected my toolbox from the kitchen and we trudged back to the truck.

"I saw lights in the house," Little Donny said. "Don't tell me you two broke in."

"All right, I won't." I hadn't planned on telling him anyway.

"You're going to have to get out and push," I said to him after I'd been rocking the truck back and forth like I'd watched Barney do. Every time I spun the tires, we slid sideways a foot or two. We needed to go backwards but it wasn't happening.

Little Donny looked down at his fancy tassel shoes and sighed. Then he opened the door and stepped out into the snow.

He threw his weight against the truck and I revved the engine. Over and over we tried. Finally Little Donny stood up and panted, "Granny, are you sure you have it in reverse?"

I looked at the gear stick. "Oops," I said, moving it from neutral to reverse.

A few more tries and we were out.

"Looks like a snowplow ran around their yard," Cora Mae pointed out as we swung into the road.

Little Donny ran up covered with dirty snow from the knees down.

"Next time you better wear more practical clothes," I said to him. Then I remembered that Little Donny wasn't exactly a willing conspirator. I dug through the glove compartment for paper napkins and helped him wipe off his shoes. Little Donny's a good boy and a great grandson. I'd have to think of a way to make this up to him.

———

We arrived at the pastie dinner as the Lionesses were beginning to clear away the food. The pasties were still out so we helped ourselves. A lot of people who aren't from the U.P. don't know what pasties are. Little Donny's city-slick father thought they were something strippers wore on their boobs. I wanted to ask him how he knew what strippers wore, but Heather was sitting right next to him at the time, and since I'm the last one to make trouble in a family I kept my mouth shut.

Pasties are a staple of life in the U.P., like bread or rice, and the Lionesses make the best found anywhere. A small wad of dough is rolled out like a piecrust, only smaller, then it's filled with chopped carrots, potatoes, onions, ground beef, and a little salt and pepper. Fold the crust over, crimp the side closed with a fork, and bake it for an hour or so. Of course, everyone has a secret ingredient they add to the mix to make theirs special. The Lionesses are sworn to secrecy and not one of them has spilled the beans yet. I'm thinking of joining just so I can find out what they do to make theirs so good.

Little Donny stacked three on his plate and sat down with a cup of coffee at an empty table. Cora Mae and I took one each and followed him over. I noticed the long metal tables were cleared of people, everyone gathered on the opposite side of the room next to a barrel of beer.

I could see Star across the room hanging on a short stocky fellow with dark wavy hair.

"Who's that with your Aunt Star?" I asked Little Donny.

"Some guy she met in Rapid River."

No wonder I hadn't seen much of her lately. Star's enjoying her freedom, but it sure took awhile. I'm proud of her for not jumping into a steady relationship with the first guy who paid her a little attention. A lot of women would do that, but Star's taking her time. "He looks like a young one. How old do you think he is?"

Little Donny shrugged his shoulders. He packed the last of the pasties in his mouth, picked up his plate, and went off in the direction of the kitchen to find more.

I saw Bill Lampi standing next to Floyd, sipping a glass of beer. He wore a proud smile like Barney used to wear when one of his kids did something special, like winning a spelling bee or scoring the winning basket in a basketball game. Only Bill smiled at the crowd of guys gathered around Barb. His smile seemed to say, "That's mine, fellas. Pretty great stuff, hunh?"

A lot of men wouldn't like their wives getting the kind of attention Barb was getting. Maybe somewhere in Bill's mind he felt lucky to have her. He probably didn't do too much dating when he was growing up.

I just hoped he didn't have more than he could handle.

I could hear dishes clattering in the kitchen and a swelling din from the other side of the room.

"Little Donny must be eating his way through the kitchen," I said to Cora Mae when he didn't return. "Let's go mingle. And keep your ears open."

We left our plates at the kitchen window and joined the crowd. The first person we saw turned out to be Kitty. She wore a housedress covered with pink flowers the size of watermelons, and I caught a glimpse of her dead-white lumpy inner thighs, although I tried hard not to. She had taken the bobby pins out of her hair, but as usual forgot to comb it out. Tight corkscrew curls bounced on her head as she leaned into a group of women ranging in size from chubby to tubby.

I recognized them as Kitty's card bunch. They got together every Friday night for rummy. Should be playing Old Maid, I thought. Not a one of them had ever been married except Pat, and that lasted only three weeks so it didn't really count.

Kitty looked directly into my eyes. Then she bent over and said something to Betty, who had taken time out from busy-bodying at Chester's door to see who else's husband she could try to steal.

Betty gasped and covered her mouth with her hand, and the group all began to giggle and glance over at me.

"Hi, Kitty." I ambled over. "Hi, girls."

Kitty turned her head away.

I had managed to make Kitty mad at me and now I had to pay my dues as the central topic of gossip. Great. "I'm sorry about earlier. I don't know what got into me," I said, certain that a public apology would do the trick. I tacked on the clincher. "I'll get you something to eat from the kitchen. Would you like that?"

Kitty beaming face swung back. "I'm okay. I'll catch up with you in a few minutes."

I sighed. "No hurry. Take the night off. I don't need a body-guard in a crowd like this."

I nudged Cora Mae and nodded in Onni's direction. "Look. There's Onni Maki."

Cora Mae barely glanced at him. "I've changed my mind about Onni. He's not what he appeared at first. Besides, he's a murder suspect and a cheater. I've heard more stories about his cheating than I care to. Believe it or not, I have my principles. I've got bigger fish to fry."

Cora Mae was making love eyes at someone behind me. I turned to look and saw George talking to old Ed Lacken.

"Good God, Cora Mae, not the undertaker." Just the thought of Ed touching a living woman made me feel sick.

"Of course not. I mean George. Isn't he cute?"

Well, doesn't that beat all? Cora Mae is a living wonder, and I can hardly keep up with her. George better watch his goods, because once Cora Mae sets her sights, it's usually too late to get away. I felt a twinge inside, not sure I liked this new development.

Cora Mae wrenched loose from my grip and slithered over to him, finding her way through a clearing in the mass of people crowded around the beer. I joined her next to George.

Ed Lacken wore the same bow tie he wore for his funeral services and every hair on his head was slicked straight back. I wondered how he kept his head from sliding off the pillow at night. He ran his fingers around the bow tie as though it pinched his neck.

Cora Mae batted her eyelashes, laid a hand on George's arm to get his attention, batted her eyes some more, and said, "I need some advice on repairing my fence. I'd appreciate it if you'd stop by tomorrow and take a look at it."

I couldn't believe anyone could be so bold and obvious. Now we have to break Cora Mae's fence.

"Sure," George said innocently. "I'll look at it first thing in the morning. Then I'm heading to Gertie's place to work on a few things." He smiled at me and I felt my face heating up.

The sound of laughter caught our attention, and we all looked over at the gang gathered around Barb.

"I think," George said slowly, "Bill has a wild cat by the tail."

While we focused on the tight circle around Barb, Onni Maki walked up and stood next to me, wearing the same green disco suit he'd worn to Chester's funeral. He wasn't standing there three seconds before I felt a hand on my rear end. I jumped and moved forward a step. The hand followed. Glancing over my shoulder, I couldn't help noticing it was Onni's hand. We looked at each other. He had a blank dumb expression on his face. I could feel his fingers spread out over one whole cheek.

I slowly opened my purse, passing up the stun gun with a pang of regret and wrapping my hand around the can of pepper spray. Then I sprayed it in Onni's face.

It was a direct hit.

He blew back like he'd been hit full force by a tornado. When he hit the floor, he covered his face and started screaming. Boy, that stuff really works.

I didn't choose the stun gun because I didn't want to cause a big scene, but with Onni screaming and the whole place turning and heading over, I might as well have. I eased the pepper spray back into my purse and edged away from the group forming around Onni, still on his back. Out of the corner of my eye I saw Blaze rushing through the crowd, and I got myself tucked back behind George just in time. I peered out.

"What the hell happened?" Blaze asked the crowd. Everyone looked at each other. I looked at Kitty, who had plowed through to stand beside me, and shrugged along with the rest of them. Blaze bent over Onni and helped him up.

"I'm blind," Onni screamed.

"There, there," Blaze said. "You just got a little something in your eye."

Onni continued screaming as Blaze guided him to the men's room. I wandered in the opposite direction before the crowd started comparing notes and looking around for the perpetrator.

I leaned against a pile of jackets in the coatroom and closed my eyes. When I opened them, Barb sashayed in like one of those fancy New York models on a catwalk, her hands on her hips and a sour look on her face.

"I need to talk to you," she said.

"Suits me."

"I want to know why you're bothering Bill and me. I know you were sneaking around outside our house spying on us, but I don't know why."

I never liked the word "sneak," but I let it ride. And I didn't like her tone of voice. Up close I noticed a tired edge to her face, like she'd been losing sleep, and I decided to cut to the chase.

"Someone broke into Chester's house," I said. "And tore it apart looking for something, and I'm pretty sure it was you."

Her face crumpled and her voice went limp. "That's why you're snooping around? You think I did that?"

"That's right," I said.

Barb looked around. No one was nearby. "Promise you won't tell Bill what I'm going to tell you, or anybody else, for that matter. Promise and I'll tell you."

She wrung her hands and chewed the bottom of her lip.

"I promise," I said. We used to call them "toilet paper promises" because they were the kind of promises that lasted about as long as one piece of toilet paper. Another price one pays to be an investigator.

"Chester found out something about me that Bill didn't know about, and after he died, I worried that Bill would go over and discover it." She paused and glanced at the door. "I went there, but I didn't have to break in. The back door was standing open and someone had already searched through everything. Chester's belongings were thrown every which way. I looked around but whoever was there ahead of me must have taken the thing I was looking for, because I couldn't find it."

Her voice started to crack and I thought she was about to cry, but she didn't.

"What were you looking for?" I asked, but of course I knew. The magazines I had discovered in Chester's blind.

"I can't tell you that. It's too embarrassing, something foolish I did years ago and regret every day of my life. Chester told me he had it and threatened to show it to Bill if I didn't go back where I came from."

"Sounds like a motive for murder to me," I said.

Barb narrowed her eyes, back to her old self.

"Where were you opening day of hunting season around dawn?" I asked her.

"You just don't quit, do you?" she said.

Little Donny wandered into the coatroom sucking on a toothpick and Barb used his presence as an opportunity to escape.

I called to her as she strutted out, "Don't leave town until this matter is resolved."

I've always wanted to say that.

———

Not one to put all my guinea hen eggs in one basket, I knew it was time to expand the scope of my investigation. There was a distinct possibility that Barb wasn't the murderer. I wanted her to be my prime suspect because she wasn't a local and because I didn't like her. But, the evidence wasn't stacking against her.

If Barb told me the truth, Chester's place had been searched three separate times the day after he bought the big one: by Cora Mae and me, by whoever trashed his place, and by Barb. Who searched my house? Not Barb or she would have taken the magazines. And who put the rifle back in Chester's gun case?

I looked around for Kitty and finally found her in the ladies' room washing her hands.

"Barb didn't do it," I said. "And Onni didn't do it because he didn't have anything to gain."

Kitty studied me in the mirror. "Sounds reasonable."

"That leaves Bill. Or we are barking up the wrong tamarack tree altogether?"

"They just took Onni to the hospital in Escanaba," Kitty said, still watching me in the mirror.

"What's wrong with him?" I squirmed, wondering how a little shot of pepper spray could require hospitalization. Those cans should have warnings.

"No one knows. Ed Lacken said Onni was standing by you one minute and screaming the next. Funny thing."

Kitty watched me in the mirror. My curls were beginning to flatten to my head. I fluffed them with my fingers and said, "Little Donny's going to need a ride home tonight. Ask George to take him and meet me by the door. I'll get the truck."

Kitty nodded.

The emergency room desk attendant was solid, like a refrigerator. She wore a fuzzy black mustache over her lip and thick black eyebrows.

"Only next of kin beyond this point," she said.

"I'm his wife." I tried to look worried.

She scanned a clipboard. "Doesn't say he has a wife on his intake sheet."

"He's not thinking right. I'm definitely his wife, though."

"Okay, but they . . ." Refrigerator pointed at Cora Mae and Kitty, "will have to wait here." Cora Mae shrugged and took a seat by the television. Kitty positioned herself for a view down the hall, leaning against the wall, a hint of garter protruding below her housedress.

I walked down a long corridor with Fridge leading the way. She wore hospital white shoes and white stretch pants that showed the lines of a pair of size eighteen panties. The panties were black.

We entered a room with three beds partitioned by curtains. She pulled aside the first one, waved me through, and thundered away to man the fort.

Onni was lying on an examination table still wearing his green suit and paisley shirt. The shirt, unbuttoned halfway, exposed his plucked-chicken wrinkly chest. He held a white cloth over both eyes.

I peeked out of the curtain to make sure no one was coming, then said in the gruffest voice I could manage, "Onni Maki, I have a few questions for you before the doctor comes in."

Startled, Onni began to lift the cloth. I quickly shoved his hand back and said, "Better not open 'em yet."

"Who are you?" Onni asked from under the cloth.

"FBI." I improvised as I went. "We're investigating the death of Chester Lampi, and this assault on you might be tied in."

"No," Onni began, "that lunatic Gert."

"Let's not go pointing fingers yet," I broke in. "This is way more complicated than it seems, and it involves land and mineral rights and greed."

"I don't have any stake in the land anymore," Onni said. "Wish everybody would leave me alone about it. I don't take to threats." Sweat glistened on his chrome-dome and a long strand of cover-up hair had slid down the side of his face.

"Nobody's threatening you."

"Yeah, right."

"Have you noticed any unusual activity over there?" I asked.

"What? Where?"

"On the land next to your place. Chester's land."

Onni seemed surprised. "That's vacant land and it's November. What kind of stupid question is that?"

Interrogation work is harder than it looks. The interrogatee might know valuable information without even knowing it. It's the interrogator's job to ask the right questions, even though the questions might seem stupid to someone not acquainted with the procedure.

"I'm asking the questions here, remember?" My throat was getting sore. "Who else has been asking about the land?"

"It doesn't matter," Onni said, "I don't have anything to do with the land or the mineral rights anymore."

"We need it for our records."

"Well, to begin with, Barb Lampi wanted to buy the rights from me, but I told her I didn't own them anymore, that I'd traded them . . ."

The curtains parted and the doctor entered, followed by Blaze, who sipped from a cup of coffee.

"Ma," Blaze said, "what are you doing here?"

Onni screamed, threw the cloth aside, and tried to open his eyes. "What's she doing here? Get her away from me!"

"That's no way to treat a visitor," I said. Blaze had me in his elbow lock and we headed down the hall.

"Bye, Mrs. Maki," Fridge called when we walked by. I waved.

Blaze stared hard to me and said, "Mrs. Maki? You impersonated a dead woman? Where's Little Donny?"

"He was having such a good time, I let him stay for the dance."

Cora Mae came trotting over. "I'm keeping an eye on her," she said. "And so is Kitty." I could see Kitty attempting to launch herself from a waiting room chair.

"Oh, good," Blaze said. "Now I won't worry anymore." He towered over me. "Onni said you squirted something in his face."

"Don't know where he got that idea. Viagra must be affecting his mind. I read that stuff can make everything look blue. Imagine what it's doing to his mind."

"I'm staying to make sure he's okay," Blaze said. "You better hope he doesn't want to press charges."

On the way out the revolving door Cora Mae said, "Spraying Onni in the face sure isn't going to help your case. Can't you save outrageous behavior till after the hearing?"

"Good point, Cora Mae, but I wasn't thinking about the case while Onni pawed me up. It was instinct."

We waited outside for Kitty to catch up. I filled them in on my conversation with Onni. "Barb's back on my list."

"I thought women didn't murder men with rifles." Cora Mae said. "Didn't you say that?"

"She must have an accomplice," I reasoned. "That's the only explanation."

"Bill," Cora Mae and Kitty said in unison.

ELEVEN

Word for the Day
CHTHONIC (THAHN ik) adj.
Designating or of the underworld of
the dead or its gods or spirits.

THURSDAY MORNING BROUGHT A warm spell. As I woke up in
Cora Mae's guest room I could hear melted snow running in the
gutters along the roof of her house. It sounded like a waterfall as
it emptied with a rush onto the side lawn and traveled toward an
irrigation ditch next to the road. An icicle broke loose from the
roofline and sailed past the window.

Kitty came over early to help with the investigation. With the
narrowing focus on Barb and Bill, I gave her a list of phone calls
to make and places to visit, and expected it would keep her busy
all day.

I wrote my word for the day on a scrap of paper and wondered
how I was going to incorporate this one into a normal conversation.

"What are you doing?" Kitty said, eyeing the dictionary.

"Nothing." I balled the paper in my hand.

"We'll make the phone calls later," Cora Mae said to Kitty. "Let's go."

Kitty, reluctant to leave me alone, refused to leave until I reminded her that she had backup. "Little Donny's on his way over. He'll protect me today."

At eight-thirty A.M. Little Donny appeared at the door, a grumpy look on his face. "How am I going to get any hunting done if I have to follow you around all day?"

I glanced at my watch. "You could have had two hours of hunting in before you came over here. You're going to have to reset your internal clock."

"I have to go home tomorrow. Mom called last night to tell me I had a response on one of my job applications. First thing Monday morning, I have an interview." Little Donny didn't appear to be jumping with joy.

"Come on. I'll buy you breakfast." I didn't want to think about him leaving.

We drove over to the Deer Horn Café, Stonely's one and only restaurant. The local boys like to hang out there every morning, and I decided to see what the current scuttlebutt might be.

As we drove up, I noticed the train had stopped on the tracks across from the restaurant with its headlight still on. That meant Otis Knutson was paying a visit. He passed by every week, driving his train to Lower Michigan and always ground her to a halt at the Deer Horn to say howdy.

George sat at a table with Carl Anderson and Otis.

"If you don't ask to borrow my car no more," Carl said to Little Donny, "you two can sit with us."

Everybody thought that was funny. It doesn't take much to get Finns and Swedes going. Their favorite game is mine's-bigger-than-yours. In the spring when the trout are running in the Escanaba River, it's my trout is bigger than yours. In the summer, it's my tomatoes are bigger than yours, and of course, in the late fall during hunting season, it's my buck is bigger than yours. It's the same old story, year in, year out, and it seems that everyone is in on the competition.

Carl won the my-tomato-is-bigger-than-yours last year, but he's still trying to live down the practical joke he fell for. George drove into Escanaba and picked out a big store-bought watermelon and tucked it into Carl's watermelon patch. Carl came flying into the restaurant all out of breath and bragging about the size of his watermelon. Only a fool would believe a watermelon could be full-grown ripe by the first of July, especially in Upper Michigan. They had a good time with that one.

"Who's got the biggest buck so far?" Otis asked.

"I got one has sixteen points and weighs a good two hundred pounds," Carl said.

"In your dreams, you B.S.'er." George joined in, rocking back on his chair and hooting.

"Big Buck's still running loose," Carl said, digging a toothpick in his teeth. "Eighteen points. Someone saw him yesterday, but he stayed on the edge of the woods. Wouldn't come in close enough for a shot. He didn't grow to get a rack like that by being stupid, ya know."

I ordered eggs over easy, bacon, and American fries. Little Donny wanted the same.

"I'm heading home tomorrow," Little Donny said to George. "I thought I might help you finish the hole in Granny's barn first."

"Sure," George said. "I'll stop home and get my tools. We can work on it right after I fix Cora Mae's fence."

I made a mental note to help Cora Mae break her fence right away. In all the excitement last night, she probably forgot. "She's out running errands with Kitty," I said.

"That's all right," George assured me. "She doesn't need to be home for me to fix it."

"Cora Mae doesn't like it when people come around when she's not there," I punted. "Better leave it for another day."

Otis had on his conductor hat with the pinstripes. He was born and raised in Trenary, making him homegrown, like most of the boys in the restaurant. I looked around. Not a woman in the bunch except me, and Ruthie, the owner, slaving in the back over the kitchen stove.

She brought our orders and refilled everyone's coffee cups. Wisps of hair had escaped from her bun and stuck to the sweat on her face. Seeing her reminded me of something.

"Ruthie," I said, squirting ketchup on my American fries, "remember last spring, those Lower Michigan fellows were in here trying to buy up land?"

"Ya, Gert, and nobody gave them the time of day."

Otis adjusted his conductor hat. "I was in here, too," he said. "Bunch a scary-looking characters."

"Have any of them been hanging around lately?" I asked, not addressing anyone in particular.

Carl shook his head. "Don't want no goofball survivalists movin' in here," he said. Carl owns more weapons than anyone around, and I wouldn't be surprised if he has some of them buried to keep them safe from theft and the federal government. I wondered what his definition of "survivalist" was.

"Walt Laakso was friendly with them," George said, "until everyone ganged up and talked some sense into him."

Checking his watch, Otis jumped up. "Holy cow, look at the time. I gotta run."

We heard a long steady toot on the train horn as the boxcars rattled into motion and chugged away.

I glanced up and saw George studying me. He always looked like he could see right into my brain and figure out what I was up to.

"What?" I asked him when he kept staring at me.

"You sure are a pretty sight today."

"Oh, stuff it, George." But I couldn't help blushing.

George grinned and slowly shook his head back and forth.

I walked out to the porch with him while Little Donny finished up another order of bacon and eggs. Since George was about the only person I could trust with a secret, I told him about Chester owning the piece of land next to Onni and the mineral rights, which I now owned. He listened carefully until I finished.

"That's pretty much the way I heard it from Kitty," George said.

I couldn't believe it. Did the whole town know? Once she wound up there was no stopping her. I heard about an operation you could give your dog if it yapped too much. De-barking, it's called. Maybe we could have that done to Kitty.

"The land must have something to do with Chester's murder."

"Kitty thinks someone's after gold."

"Gold," I scoffed. "The only gold involved in this case is packed in Kitty's molars."

George burst out laughing. I told him about the Ropes Gold Mine and Kitty's theory. It sounded pretty farfetched when I said it out loud.

"Just be careful, Gertie."

George had parked in the back of the restaurant next to an LP tank. We walked in that direction, dodging puddles where the snow melted.

"Maybe Chester was murdered by those fellows from Lower Michigan," I said, thinking out loud as we strolled back to his truck. "Maybe they were in cahoots with Barb."

"Sounds like a tall tale to me," George said, but he wasn't paying attention. Instead, he stood with the truck door open, hands on his hips.

"Damn," he said, "I thought I locked up."

"What's the matter?" I asked.

"My rifle's gone."

———

No one at the Deer Horn Restaurant had seen anyone hanging around back by George's truck. His rifle, which he'd laid on the floor tucked in under the seat, had walked away.

"Maybe chthonics took it," I said, not really sure I'd used my word right.

"Hunh?" George said, distractedly.

"Never mind."

"Better call Blaze," Ruthie said to George.

That was my cue to hit the road. I didn't want anything to do with the traitorous Blaze Johnson.

———

Walter Laakso was considered a hermit, even for these parts. The ruts in his private dirt road were so deep you'd think an earthquake had passed through. My truck bounced and bobbed so violently I thought we might have to get out and walk the rest of the way. I was grateful that Little Donny was driving instead of me.

"What kind of job interview?" I asked Little Donny, clutching the dash as we hit the ruts.

"An office job at an investment firm in downtown Milwaukee. I applied right before I came up here. I'd rather stay."

"You can't pass up the opportunity to make money," I said, disappointed. Little Donny didn't have his buck yet, and I hadn't spent nearly enough time with him.

We pulled up to the house and got out.

Walter met us in the dirt next to his house with a sawed-off shotgun in his hand. He raised it and beaded in on us. Little Donny hit the ground.

"Get up," I said. "Don't let Walter make a fool of you." Then to Walter, "Put that thing away. Have you gone blind? It's Gertie Johnson, and that's my grandson, Little Donny, wallowing in the mud."

Walter lowered the shotgun and squinted. "Sorry. Eyes aren't what they used to be. Come on in. Want some coffee?" Walter grinned and I could see his front teeth were missing.

"Sure."

We sat at the kitchen table while Walter made coffee in a pot on the stove. I sat on a chair with a wobbly leg, hoping it didn't give out till I was up and gone. The sink brimmed with dirty dishes and a layer of dust and food grime covered the table instead of a tablecloth. I was afraid to look down at the chair I sat on. Walter didn't look any too clean himself.

He poured a cup all around, then poured a juice glass full of brandy from an oversized bottle on the counter. I glanced at my watch. It was just past ten o'clock in the morning.

Walter sat down and poured some brandy into his coffee cup, then passed the brandy glass to Little Donny. I took a sip of my coffee and thought it was perfect. The old timers don't need fancy percolators or coffee machines to make a decent cup of coffee. They boil some water, throw in a handful of ground coffee, and let it boil away for a while—five or ten minutes, depending on how strong they like it. If the pot sits a few minutes before it's poured, the grounds settle on the bottom of the pot, making for clean, rich coffee.

"Sorry for scarin' you like that, boy."

"That's okay." Little Donny had mud all over the front of his coat. He took a gulp of the brandy and I noticed a twitch in the hand holding the juice glass.

"Walter, I'm investigating Chester's murder, and I need to ask you some questions."

"Didn't know he was murdered. Talk is he took a stray."

"We need to rule out murder, is all," I said, remembering that I knew things others didn't. "Those guys from down south last spring were trying to buy up land. They tried to buy from you, didn't they?"

"That's right."

"Did you catch their names?"

"Naw, didn't pay attention to that."

"Too bad," I said, taking another sip of coffee.

"But they ended up buying property up by St. Ignace."

"How do you know that?"

"They're friends of my brother. He keeps in touch, writes me letters once in a while."

I mentally crossed the Detroit boys off my list of suspects. An amateur investigator might be disappointed when faced with a dead-end, but for me it simply eliminated possibilities—tightening the noose, closing in.

"Chester wouldn't sell to my brother's friends, but then he turned right around and started negotiating to sell to someone else."

I slid forward. "Who else?"

"Don't know, but he said his property was as good as sold last time I talked to him. Right before he died."

"Right before he died?"

"Yup."

"Better do some work on your road," I told Walter. "My eyeballs nearly popped out of my head getting in here, and Little Donny's brains are scrambled for sure."

———

Little Donny was still driving when we passed Chester's house on the way back from Walter's, and I noticed the Lampi's foreign car in the driveway.

"Whoa," I called out. "Back up. We're paying a visit."

Little Donny swung around, turned in, and parked. Bill Lampi came to the door and watched us walk up to the house. I stepped over the broken boards on the porch. Bill opened the door and we wiped our wet boots on a worn rug.

"Thought we'd stop and see how you've been doing," I said. Bill wore a blue sweater pulled over an oxford shirt, and he wiped his hands on a dishtowel.

"I'm fine." He peered at us through his thick glasses. "I'm going through some of Dad's things, trying to put the place back together. Who would do something like this?" He gestured at the mess.

Everything Chester owned had been dumped on the floor. Bill had brought a stack of empty cardboard boxes, which he'd piled by the door, and by the looks of things, he had just started to clean up.

"I tell you what," I offered. "Why don't I stay and help for awhile. I'll clean up the kitchen."

I took the dishtowel from him and started for the kitchen. What an opportunity. And no sign of Barb. She probably didn't want to mess up her manicure by working here.

"I couldn't ask you to do this," Bill called after me.

"You didn't ask. I offered." I turned to Little Donny. "You go on. I'll call you when I'm done and you can pick me up."

Little Donny nodded and tore out of there, grateful that he wasn't being asked to help.

Chester had the smallest kitchen I'd ever seen. There was barely room to maneuver between the table and the sink. Garbage and broken dishes covered the floor. I took a garbage bag and picked up as much from the floor as I could, then ran water in the sink and started on the unwashed dishes. I had two thoughts as I worked. The first was that whoever searched the house didn't care about covering up his tracks. The second thought was that Walter Laakso would be right at home in this mess.

I noticed someone had replaced the broken glass in the back door. Bill, probably. I thought I should talk to him about the broken porch boards before I left. Those needed attention, too, before someone broke a leg.

Bill worked in the bedroom for a while, then came to check on me.

"You don't know how much I appreciate your help," he said. I could hear the relief in his voice as he saw the kitchen shaping up. He leaned on the edge of the counter, took his glasses off, laid them on the counter, and rubbed his face with both hands. "It's a lot all at once—cleaning up, sorting through Dad's boxes, trying to make sense out of something so senseless. You were right. He was murdered. The sheriff told me."

"I heard about that. What'll happen to the house now?" I asked.

"I'm not sure. Barb's family likes to hunt. They might come up once in a while and use it as a hunting cabin."

"Don't you hunt?" I asked.

"No, I was never interested in it, which I know is strange for around here." Bill picked up his glasses and put them on.

"To each his own," I said. "Your pa owned land over by Onni, didn't he?"

"Yes, but Pa kept quiet about that. I'm surprised you know."

"Nothing's a secret in Stonely," I said. "Has anyone been asking about Chester's land?"

"What do you mean?" Bill picked up a towel and began to wipe dishes and put them in the cupboard.

"Has anyone shown an interest in buying the land?" I asked.

"Why, yes. An outfit out of Chicago wanted to buy it and make it into a corporate retreat. Dad asked me to look over the contract before he signed it, but he died before he finished the deal."

Hiding my excitement I asked, "What's going to happen now?"

"Barb and I talked it over and decided to keep the land."

"Land's like gold to you?" I asked, watching his face carefully. He didn't miss a blink, not a facial muscle, not any sign of significance.

"I wanted to sell, but Barb was emphatic. We'll keep it."

Barb was worth another seriously long look.

I meant that figuratively, but glancing out the kitchen window, I saw her climbing out of a black sedan. My time was almost up.

Bill dropped the towel and headed for the bedroom. I heard him call, "Hi, Barb," as he went. "We have help. Mrs. Johnson is cleaning the kitchen."

So much for sneaking out the back.

I heard another car pull in, and watched Cora Mae and Kitty trot toward the house. Correction—Cora Mae trotted. Kitty lumbered.

Everyone met in the middle of the living room.

"What are you doing here?" Barb hissed at me, her eyes narrow slits.

"I'm helping out."

"Little Donny told us you were here," Cora Mae said to me. "We came to help." Cora Mae unbuttoned her coat and began to take it off.

Barb glanced at Cora Mae, did a double take then turned for a face-off.

"That looks like a dress I'm missing," Barb said to Cora Mae. Barb stood with her long legs spread wide and her knees slightly bent in attack mode.

I couldn't help noticing that she was right. Sure enough, Cora Mae wore the sheath dress she had admired when we'd broken into Barb's house. Cora Mae was turning out to be more of a liability than an asset.

"And just what are you implying?" Cora Mae planted herself, deciding on the denial route of defense. She wasn't going to back down.

"I'm calling the sheriff." Barb picked up the phone on Chester's end table.

I slipped on my boots without lacing them, grabbed my purse and coat, and used my body to force Cora Mae out the door. Kitty, obviously quicker in an emergency than I anticipated, had already slipped into her white rusted-out Lincoln and had turned it around when we reached it.

"Let's hit it," I said.

Kitty's tires slid in the melting snow, and the car fishtailed. Kitty spun the wheel and the car straightened out. She tore down the road, hitting the muddy puddles at full speed and sending water flying every which way.

"I thought you two were supposed to be investigating a murder," I said, clutching my purse on my lap. I glanced at Cora Mae's attire. "I didn't need any help. I had it under control, at least until you pranced in wearing stolen goods. Who's calling who outrageous?"

"Now, be nice," Cora Mae said. "We made phone calls all morning from my house. Didn't we, Kitty?"

"You left ahead of me," I reminded her.

"Well, we came right back because I forgot something."

"We called insurance companies looking for policies," Kitty said, "but that's slow going."

"I'm pretending I'm Barb," Cora Mae said. "When I call I say, 'This is Barb Lampi and I'd like to check on my father-in-law's insurance policy.'"

"No luck so far," Kitty told me.

"Forget the insurance policy. She's after the land, but why? That's the baffling part of it."

"It's the gold," Cora Mae insisted. "She's found a gold mine."

"That's hooey."

"I waited all morning for George to show up," Cora Mae pouted, revealing the real reason she went back home. "What do you think happened?"

I told her about George's missing rifle. "Besides," I said, "don't you need to break it first?"

"Kitty helped me. She backed into it with the bumper of her car and it went right over like it was made of tinker toys."

"Didn't hurt the car at all," Kitty chuckled. She passed the car ahead of us, ignoring the solid yellow line in the middle of the road.

They let me off at my house and Kitty insisted on waiting for reinforcements. Once Little Donny arrived, I shooed them away quickly before Cora Mae found out that George was on his way over.

Five minutes later George pulled in with his tools. After I cleaned up the bedroom and part of the living room, I threw my jacket back on and went out to the shed to watch. George had worked on it earlier so most of it was finished. Little Donny sat on the tractor eating sugar doughnuts out of a white paper bag. I dug in the bag and helped myself.

"Find your rifle?" I asked George.

"Someone took it. That's for sure."

Little Donny had sugar all over his face. "Why would anyone steal your rifle?"

"Bet it has something to do with Chester's murder." I answered for George. "I'm trying to connect the dotted lines but they're zig-zagging all over the place."

"Two more hours and we'll be through," George said. "Then I'm going to cut the last few trees."

Most of our Christmas trees were cut and shipped the first week in November, but George likes to save trees for family and friends until later in November. They keep better.

Watching the snow turn into slop, I had to disagree with him. "Better not cut them until it goes cold again," I said, "or all the needles will fall off for sure."

"A cold spell's coming in again," George said. "Tonight."

That's the beauty of Michigan weather. You don't like it today, don't worry, it'll change again by tomorrow. A twenty- or thirty-degree swing overnight isn't unusual here. Every day's a surprise.

"I'm going out to the blind," I announced.

I got my shotgun out of the hall closet and filled my pockets with shells. It must be force of habit, since I had no intention of actually hunting. I take out a license every year so a DNR agent won't come along and wonder what I'm doing in a hunting blind without one. They're a suspicious bunch.

The hunting license reminded me to make an appointment soon to take a driving test. I'd have to do it eventually.

It was almost too warm for my orange hunting jacket, but only a fool would run around in the woods during deer season without one. I compromised and left my hunting cap on a chair. Orange hair was good enough.

Looking around at my kitchen, I began planning to move back in. Mary and Little Donny had worked hard to put it back together. A few hours of effort on my part and a little shopping and it would be good as new.

I looked out at the apple tree and pondered digging up my money box before the ground froze.

———

Just thinking about being home again cheered me up. I whistled a broken tune as I plopped through the puddles on the path to the blind. After replenishing the bait pile, I kicked back without needing to start the heater and dreamed of Barney.

Barney visited often in the fourteen months since his death, and I was used to it now, even welcomed it. Instead of his being old, like he was when he died, in my dreams he was like he was when we first were married. He was lean and muscular, and he had a dimple in his left cheek when he smiled. Sometimes I wonder what I look like to him in my dreams. I never see myself. Probably wrinkly with liver spots starting to pop up all over my hands and arms.

But Barney didn't seem to care how old I looked, because he smiled at me, showing his dimple. "I told you, didn't I," he said, "that you still have a whole lot of living to do." He put his arm around my shoulder and I melted into his chest. "Life's chopped up into pieces, and you and I did it all. We were young together, we raised a family, we settled in for quiet retirement years. We lived a lot of lives together and now you're carving out another life for yourself, an independent one."

If I were a cat, I would have purred. "I was always independent. Never needed you a day in my life, you old coot, but I wanted you. I always wanted you."

We sat that way awhile, not saying anything, and then he faded.

When I woke up it was getting cold in the blind, and I regretted not firing up the stove. I rubbed my eyes and when I looked out the window, I saw movement on the deer trail. Something moved toward the bait pile, hugging the pines. I leaned forward in my chair to get a good look. When it came out into the clearing, I saw that it wasn't a deer, but a person dressed in brown work clothes.

At first I thought it was Cora Mae. Only Cora Mae is dumb enough to trot through the woods dressed like a deer. I suppose during bear season she'll do woods walks in her fake black fur, too. And she wore Kitty's black facemask. When I noticed the rifle resting in the crook of one arm, I knew it wasn't her. Cora Mae hadn't held a weapon once in her whole life.

I stood up and opened the door to call out, but the cobwebs were clearing and I remembered how warm it was outside. Even with the temperature beginning to drop, a facemask was overkill.

He came purposefully toward the blind. Skirting the bait pile, he raised the rifle and fired wildly at me without taking good aim. Wood splintered next to my head, and I jumped back inside, slamming the door. My hand came away from my forehead bloody. *God, I've been hit,* was my first thought, but then I took a better guess and decided the blood was the result of wood slivers. I was pretty sure I wouldn't be standing taking inventory if I'd been hit. That wasn't a toy rifle.

Nobody thinks to put a lock on the inside of a deer shack, but I wished I had one now. I grabbed my shotgun just as another shot penetrated the blind. I could see where it entered next to the window and exited the blind over my head.

Maybe Barney was wrong about me having a whole lot of living to do. He should have been able to see this coming and warned me ahead of time. Instead I was going out the same way Chester went out—quiet and quick.

The next shot came in. I heard it at the same time I saw the hole in the wood. With a thud it took out a piece of the back of my hunting chair. My ears rang.

The blind measured six feet by six feet, which meant the shooter was bound to hit me if he kept it up. I had three choices. I could keep dodging around inside hoping he'd run out of ammo before he clobbered me. I call it the sitting-duck plan. Or I could lie down on the floor where I'd be safe from the rifle, but then he could just walk in and finish me off. The roll-over-and-play-dead plan. Or I could try to out-fire-power him. I chose number three.

Just because I'm getting old doesn't mean I'm ready to lie down and call it quits.

Peeking through a porthole, I aimed in the direction I'd last seen him and emptied a pocket of shells. I heard rustling in the brush, and I grabbed another box of shells from a shelf on the wall. I fired the entire box. That's a lot of shells. He'd gotten off a few rounds when I first started firing back, but hadn't made a peep since.

I listened for movement and noticed my hands shook. Sweat ran down the side of my cheek and I wondered where Little Donny and George were. They must have heard the shooting.

Blood dripped into my eyes. I used my sleeve to wipe it away. The silence pounded in my ears louder than anything I've ever heard. My heart hammered in my head.

I looked down at the empty boxes at my feet and knew I had only one more chance. One shell left, and I was saving it.

I couldn't decide if the shooter was any good or not. I know he took Chester out with one bullet right between the eyes, but he seemed to be having some trouble targeting in on me. That first wild shot he fired proved he could get overanxious and miss. He seemed to need the element of surprise, and this wasn't a surprise anymore.

I decided to make a run for it if my last bullet missed its mark. I glanced down at my heavy hunting boots and sighed. I remembered the deed, tucked into the chair, and felt around for it, keeping one eye trained on the window. The paper crunched against my fingers and I pulled it out. No one would ever find it in the blind, and if I died, I wanted my family to know it existed.

It was why I might die in the next few minutes. I was certain of it.

I stuffed it into my boot.

Movement in the brush on the opposite side of the blind caught my eye. I swung the shotgun and sighted in, careful not to shoot wild and waste my last shell. I saw orange, then George's voice calling, "Gert, are you okay?"

"Careful," I yelled. "Someone's out there with a rifle."

"I think he's gone," George shouted.

"I'm not so sure."

"I heard a car engine start down on the logging road. He's gone."

George was still cautious coming in. I opened the blind door and held onto the door for balance. George took my arm. "I was over by the Christmas trees and heard all the firing. What's going on?"

My legs, reduced to soft rubber, wouldn't support me. "Get me out of here. I'll tell you later." I thought we better get out of the woods as soon as possible in case the shooter returned.

I heard Little Donny call out and his hulking form came into view.

After handing my gun to George, I mustered the last of my courage and managed to walk out under my own power.

———

Everyone milled around asking questions all at once. I was slouched on Blaze's couch, an ice pack pressed against my forehead, when I heard Blaze pull into the driveway, lights and siren.

He ran for the house, forgetting to turn off the strobe lights. In the gathering dusk, they spun through the room like carnival lights.

Mary and George moved aside to let him through. He sat down next to me and examined my forehead while I told him what had happened.

"George went back with Carl and Little Donny and poked around," I finished. "They found George's missing rifle thrown down on the deer trail."

"Looks like whoever he is doesn't have his own weapon," Blaze mumbled, deep in thought. "I'm going to need that rifle, George."

"It's out in my truck. I wore gloves picking it up and only handled it by the barrel. Maybe you can lift some prints."

"He was wearing gloves," I said. "You're probably wasting your time."

"Ma, I told you to butt out a long time ago. You almost got yourself killed." Blaze wrote in his notebook, his fat fingers with the chewed-down nails scribbling away.

"I'm obviously doing a better job than you are," I answered smugly. "They aren't vandalizing *your* place and shooting at *you*."

"Was it a man or a woman?" Blaze asked the same question everyone else asked and got the same reply.

"I don't know. At first I just assumed it was a man, but thinking back, I'm not sure. It's possible it could have been a woman who knows how to handle a rifle."

"Did you notice anything unusual?"

"Not unless you call dressing up to look like an animal during gun hunting season and firing at an innocent woman unusual."

Mary used tweezers to pull out shards of wood embedded in my scalp and forehead. The ice pack had done its job—I didn't feel a thing. A piece of gauze taped across the wound, a few pain killers, and tomorrow I'd be good as new.

Mary insisted that George and I stay for supper. We had pork chops, parsley boiled potatoes, canned beans from Mary's garden, and for dessert we had Jell-O with little pieces of fruit in it. You would have thought after my near-death experience I wouldn't be hungry, but I did just fine. Being almost killed works up a person's appetite.

After supper George drove me to my house to pick up my truck and followed me over to Cora Mae's. Blaze argued with me over my plan, wanting me to stay with him, but I resisted, not aiming to give him any ammunition for the court hearing. I'd had enough of ammo for one night.

Circumstances had forced me to temporarily set aside my differences with Blaze. Our meeting tonight had been strictly professional. Tomorrow I would go back to disowning him.

Before I went to bed I put the stun gun on the battery charger.

TWELVE

Word for the Day
PROMULGATING (PRAHM uhl GAY teng) v.
Making widespread.

"I NEED YOU AND Cora Mae to check every gun shop between here and Escanaba." Kitty and I sat at Cora Mae's kitchen table early Friday morning. Cora Mae was making buttermilk pancakes from a box mix.

Six inches of fresh, heavy snow had fallen through the night, and it was still snowing. Cora Mae and I took turns brushing the accumulation from her front steps with a broom.

"We're promulgating this case," I said, in a hurry to use my word for the day and get it over with.

"We're what?" Cora Mae wanted to know.

Kitty piped up before I could answer. "We're expanding our search for the killer," she explained.

I shook my head. Where was she learning these words?

183

Kitty didn't seem to think anything of it. She acted like she used big words every day. I watched her suck in pancakes without chewing.

"See what rifles are in the shops for repair," I said. "Someone's helping themselves to a lot of weapons, and I can't figure out why. Maybe a name will jump out at you."

"We can go through the yellow pages," Kitty said. "There can't be too many gun repair shops."

"You better go to them. Maybe Cora Mae can weasel information out of them that they wouldn't give on the phone." I sipped my coffee and tried to ignore my head, which throbbed from yesterday's wound. "Every hardware store repairs guns. Hit every last one of them."

Kitty shifted her weight. "This is serious business now. Someone tried to kill you. No more fun and games. We have to get the killer before he gets you."

"Let's go over the facts one more time," I said, flipping open my notebook. "Chester's family wins Onni's family land in a poker game, but Onni retains the mineral rights. Chester's ready to sell the land to an outfit from Chicago, but is murdered before he can complete the deal. The desperate killer rips apart Chester's house and my house and we have to assume he's looking for the mineral rights, which suddenly I own."

I glanced up. "Right so far."

"Right," Kitty and Cora Mae said in unison.

"The killer," I continued, "steals George's rifle and uses it to attempt to kill me. According to Onni, when Barb tried to buy the mineral rights from him, he told her I owned them. And finally, Bill said Barb wouldn't let him sell the land."

I dropped the notebook on the table. "This is all adding up."

"And?" Cora Mae leaned expectantly over the table.

"It's obvious, Cora Mae," I said. "Barb has a motive; she didn't want the land sold. And she had the opportunity to steal Chester's rifle and kill him. We have our killer. And to think I almost believed her."

"Killers are smooth talkers," Kitty said, like she really knew anything about murderers.

While we were eating pancakes, Little Donny walked in dressed in hunter's orange. He settled at the table and Cora Mae slapped a stack of pancakes on his plate.

"Blaze is driving me to the airport this afternoon," he said through a mouthful. "I'm heading back to Milwaukee."

"I'm sure going to miss you," I said to Little Donny. "It's been great fun, even if you didn't get your buck. Plan on coming next September for bear season. That's always a good time."

"Sounds like a plan," Little Donny said, butter dripping from his chin.

The phone rang and Cora Mae picked it up. Listening to her one-sided conversation, I knew she was talking to Blaze.

"A robber? Impossible. . . . Me? . . . Well, it's my word against hers and I say I didn't do it. . . . Can't two people own the same dress? Hers wasn't the only one made, you know."

Cora Mae had her free hand on her hip and rolled her eyes for our benefit. "Kitty's license plate number on the getaway car? You'll have to talk to her about that." She listened again then covered the receiver and said to me, "Blaze wants to talk to you."

"I'm not here."

"She's not here," Cora Mae said into the phone and hung up.

Little Donny stayed until the box of pancake mix was empty then gave goodbye hugs all around.

I slipped on my boots and jacket, and walked with him to Blaze's Buick. "Maybe you can come for Christmas. Tell Heather to come, too."

"Depends on whether or not I have a job."

I nodded and waved as he drove off. Snow the size of cotton balls plopped down in fluffy piles, and I swept the porch one more time before going back in.

Kitty had a theory waiting for me inside.

"I think George is the killer," she said, casually dropping her bombshell.

I almost spit coffee. "That's a good one."

Kitty didn't smile. "And I think George tried to kill you. He knew you weren't home the night of the break in."

"But he was with me the entire time, playing cards. He has an iron-clad alibi."

"He's the accomplice."

"And whose accomplice would he be?"

"Barb Lampi's," Kitty said.

Cora Mae's eyes grew wide and she gasped. "A love triangle."

"No." I snorted. "A love triangle would be between George, Barb, and Bill. Bill would be dead, not Chester."

"You're right."

"Where was George while you were fighting for your life in the blind?" Kitty asked.

"Cutting Christmas trees."

"Where was Little Donny?"

"I don't know." I frowned in thought, remembering that Little Donny came from the direction of the house and George had come from the tree line. "Working in the barn maybe."

"You don't know where George was," Kitty said, slowly. "But you know who owned the rifle."

I felt the color drain out of my face. "George's rifle was stolen."

"Was it? George had time to attack you, hide the clothes he wore, and pop out of the woods as good old George, your friend."

"This can't be true," I muttered.

"A horrible thought just raced through my head." Cora Mae squealed. "What if it *is* true and Little Donny showed up before he could finish the job? I think Little Donny might have saved your life."

Kitty slapped her thighs. "There you go."

The more I thought about it, the more ridiculous it sounded.

Kitty shifted again and the chair groaned. "George and Barb could be lovers, driven by greed for the land and the promise of gold. George knew he had to kill you before you exposed his scheme. You haven't been telling him about our investigation, have you?"

I shuddered, remembering. "I might have told him a little."

"You have to learn to keep a secret," Loudspeaker Kitty had the nerve to say. "It could be the difference between life and death."

"Every time I'm interested in somebody they turn out to be a prime suspect in this murder case." Cora Mae said.

"You do go through them quickly," Kitty observed, while I studied her.

"Well," I said. "This new murder theory was a lot of fun, but let's get back to real life now and work on this case. George is no more a murderer than I am a . . ." I struggled with a comparison.

". . . a fashion model," Cora Mae finished for me with a howl.

Kitty tilted her chair back onto two legs, I saw a slight wobble, and Kitty, in slow motion, sank to the floor.

"Legs snapped right off the chair," she puffed as we helped her up and resettled her in a sturdier chair.

I couldn't help noticing Kitty's new wardrobe accessories. "Where did you find white bobby pins?"

"A hairdresser friend of mine. You like them?"

"Snazzy," I said.

A few minutes later Kitty and Cora Mae squealed out of the driveway in Kitty's rusted-out beater, hot on the trail of the man they insisted had only pretended to be my friend.

"Don't forget Barb," I called after them. "My money's on her."

A few minutes after that, they were back at the house.

"Almost forgot my job," Kitty said sheepishly after climbing the steps one more time and resting. "You have to come with us if I'm going to protect you. I messed up once, I'm not about to do it again."

"You can drop me at my appointment."

———

The psychological evaluator put me through what he called "a battery of tests," including the old standard inkblots. They were easy.

"Doughnuts," I said when he asked me to use my imagination. "Tractor tires, blow flies."

I tried to explain to him that I didn't have time for all this nonsense; I had a bigger goose to cook. But he insisted that the court would expect the results of these specific tests.

After the written and visual tests, he wanted to talk about me and about what was going on in my life.

He was taller than anyone I'd ever met. When he first opened the door, I thought I'd walked into the Green Giant's lair. He was well over six-foot-five.

Cora Mae won't date a tall man. She says she's always looking up into his nose hairs and there's always something suspicious dangling there. The psychologist's nose hairs were fine.

He pushed back from the table and wrapped his long legs in a complicated twist like a pretzel and waited for me to begin.

I gave him an earful.

I told him about the murder investigation, the attempts on my life, the suspects, and about the document in Barney's notebook. In fact, I showed him the deed, which was the only piece of concrete evidence I had in my possession. I did have the shot-up hunting blind, but that's more stationary evidence. I offered to show him that, too, if he felt like taking a drive. He said it wouldn't be necessary.

He listened without interrupting, making notes as I talked. I leaned forward, trying to read the notes upside down, but he moved the papers away.

When I was finished he said, "Uh huh."

And that was his entire contribution to our conversation and his only comment on all the information I'd presented him with.

"Has Blaze been in for his evaluation yet?" I wanted to know on the way out the door.

"It's not required for him."

"Figures," I said. The ones who need it never have to. "Did I pass?"

"I'll be issuing a report and you will receive a copy."

I better have passed or I'm in deep trouble.

———

Cora Mae and Kitty escorted me back to Cora Mae's house.

"I didn't realize how many shops repair guns," Cora Mae whined. "They're in Trenary, Gladstone, Escanaba, and a few places scattered here and there between Rapid River and Marquette."

"Forget Rapid River and Marquette. No one from around here would drive all that way."

"Well, we're about half done."

"Put it on hold for awhile. We need to follow George and tie him in with Barb."

Both stared at me.

"I'm not saying you're right," I said with regret. "But he's on the list. The very bottom of the list."

Kitty had a sack of Big Macs, fries, and chocolate shakes from Escanaba. We warmed the burgers and fries in the microwave and dug in.

"I'm having a lot of trouble believing that George is a killer," I said between mouthfuls. "He's been my best friend . . ."

Cora Mae gave me a withering look.

"I mean, after you, of course. And he's been so nice to me, doing repairs, playing cards; I can't believe it."

Kitty started in on her second Big Mac. I've never seen anyone eat two Big Macs in my entire life. "Killers look and act just like the rest of us," she said.

"Give me one good reason why George would want to kill me."

"You have an unregistered deed to the mineral rights on three hundred acres of prime land that Bear Creek runs right through and that could possibly be the site of a huge vein of precious metal," Kitty said with one cheek full of fries.

"When you say it like that," I said, "it sounds believable."

Cora Mae chimed in. "I always knew something was strange about him."

"You did not." I rubbed my hands together to shake off the bun crumbs. "And answer this for me—if I can't register the rights because I'm dead, then they still belong to Onni, not to Barb or George. Are they going to kill him too? And then what? Who are Onni's heirs? Are they going to kill all of them?"

We all traded surprised expressions.

"Who would inherit Onni's estate?" Kitty put special sarcastic emphasis on the word *estate*. "He doesn't have any family, at least that we know of."

"It doesn't matter because his distant relatives would probably sell it for next to nothing." I was on a roll. "Onni's in as much danger as I am. We're both marked for execution."

"What should we do, Gertie?" Cora Mae asked. "What's our next step?"

"Surveillance run tonight, partners."

———

Owning the mineral rights to Chester's land means I own everything under the ground, dirt and all. Does that mean I can haul away the topsoil? There are quite a few gray areas associated with these rights. and I need to find the answers. For now, I know I own the following things if, and this is a big if, they are found—oil, copper, iron ore, silver, or gold. Quite an impressive list of valuables.

Another thing I know—gold is found along streambeds just like Bear Creek, which runs through said land. And gold really has been found in Marquette County, which is close enough to almost spit on. And the U.P. is part of the Canadian Shield, made up of the oldest rock in the world. And oil has even been discovered here, so why is the idea of gold farfetched?

Ropers Gold Mine, according to the librarian in Escanaba, had the richest specimens of gold-bearing quartz ever found in the area, and every river in Michigan has had shows of gold.

Gold in the ground, in my ground? It's not nearly as impossible as I thought. My scoffing days are over.

———

Surveillance work isn't as glamorous as most people think. Every time I tell someone I'm an investigator they want to know about the spying part of it.

For one thing, it's dangerous. The last thing you want is your suspect walking up to your vehicle and confronting you. There's nothing worse than being hauled out by your shirt collar and held ten inches off the ground while he waits for a plausible explanation.

It could happen.

What's more likely to happen, though, is the neighbors get suspicious, think you're spying on them, and call the police. Then there's some explaining to do, especially if it's late at night, which is when the most serious surveillance work is carried on.

Finding the right spot to watch from isn't easy, either. Once the suspect starts moving, you don't know which way he'll go. You need perfect positioning.

You also need a bucket of Kentucky Fried Chicken, which Kitty brought, a six-pack of Pepsi, and an old rusty coffee can, which I provided. Just in case. You can't go looking for a bathroom in the middle of your watch. He'll decide to move exactly then.

I still couldn't believe George would murder Chester, but the evidence tipped heavily in his direction. And stronger men than George have succumbed to the wiles of a woman. I remember hearing that George's wife ran off a while back, maybe six or seven years ago, on Christmas Eve. When George got home from work, there was a note waiting for him on the kitchen table. I thought that was a cruel way to leave someone. George never talked about her, and never took up with anyone else as far as I knew. Until now.

"Here he comes," Kitty said, already digging into the bucket, one greasy hand full of chicken poised halfway to her mouth. "Duck."

Headlights sliced the dark leading from George's house and his truck turned onto the road heading toward Stonely. Kitty started the car and blew out of the ditch, a chicken leg clenched in her jaw, both hands swinging the wheel sharply. Running without headlights to guide her, she strained forward in her seat to see.

Cora Mae clutched the bucket of chicken, a soda pop can flew from the seat, and we were in hot pursuit.

"Don't pass him up," I called out as Kitty continued to gather speed. "Stay way back."

Kitty popped on her lights when we passed through Stonely. George's truck kept going. "He's heading for Gladstone."

Twenty minutes later we drove down Delta Avenue, the main drag in Gladstone, staying back as far as possible without losing sight of him. All the little shops were along a six- or seven-block stretch and they were all closed.

George turned onto a side street, and Kitty almost rear-ended him. "He's parking," I said, ducking down. Kitty swerved around his truck and sped away.

"Did he see us?" Cora Mae said.

I straightened up. "I don't see how he could have since we were moving at the speed of light. Kitty, you have to learn the meaning of slow."

After much discussion and a little backtracking, we parked a block away from George's truck, which was now empty. We spend several minutes guessing where he might be.

Another danger in surveillance work is the risk of being recognized by the suspect or by someone passing on the sidewalk. We'd taken care of that. Cora Mae has a wig for every occasion so we all were in disguise. My wig was long and blond, Cora Mae's was a sassy little red bun, and Kitty's was a black flip, which I hear is back in style.

We had to keep the truck running because it was cold and we needed the heat. Snow still fell, heavy and wet, so occasionally Kitty ran the windshield wipers to clear the glass, the defroster barely keeping up with our warm breath.

Another danger in the eye-spy field is boredom. It's the number one reason surveillance is so difficult. Hours and hours of sitting staring out the window can drive you over the edge into insanity, or can put you right to sleep.

Cora Mae kept the conversation going.

"Do you have an attorney yet?" she asked.

"I don't need one." I brushed coarse blond hair out of my eyes.

"The judge said you did."

"I'm representing myself."

"You're not taking any advice," Cora Mae whined, "and I'm not visiting you in some nursing home in Escanaba. You need to spruce up your appearance, tone down your personality, and get a lawyer. It's only for a little while, and then you can go back to your old self."

"And you," she turned to Kitty, whose black flip was bobbing in time with her chews. "You need to spruce up, too, so you can find a man."

Kitty stopped chewing. "I can get a man anytime I want to. In fact, I fight them off daily."

Cora Mae and I looked doubtful.

"It's true. Haven't you ever heard of chubby chasers?"

Cora Mae hooted and we shushed her.

"Lots of men out there like a fat woman," Kitty said. "If you don't believe me, ask one of them." She licked her fingers. "I just don't want one."

Cora Mae's final words of advice were, "If you don't use it, you're going to lose it. It's like pierced ear holes. They close right up if you don't keep putting posts in."

"Shhh." I saw two black dots walking down Delta from the opposite direction, heading toward George's truck. I scrambled for the binoculars and put them up to my eyes. Nothing.

Apparently binoculars don't work well in the dark. Kitty tried to see through them, then Cora Mae tried. The black dots came close enough so I could make out the shadows of arms and legs, but we were parked too far away to get a good look. The falling snow and fogged windows didn't help either.

Kitty started the car and rolled forward. But it was too late. A figure came into shadowy view and hopped into the truck. Whoever he was with had vanished.

I put night-vision binoculars on my wish list.

THIRTEEN

Word for the Day
HIRSUTE (HURR soot) adj.
Hairy; shaggy; bristly.

BRIGHT AND EARLY SATURDAY morning Blaze called Cora Mae's house looking for me. "He says he knows you're here," Cora Mae called out, covering the receiver with her hand. "If you don't talk to him, he says he's coming over."

"All right," I said, reluctantly taking the phone.

"I had George and Carl keep an eye on Cora Mae's house through the night," Blaze said. "I deputized them. I'm worried sick since someone took shots at you out by the blind."

Great. Blaze has one of the prime suspects following me around with a badge and a weapon.

"I've got a deputy coming over to watch out for you until we clear this up. Where are you going to be today?"

"I don't need some pimply-faced kid chasing after me. I have Kitty."

"You don't have a choice. Where can he count on finding you? He'll be out in the next hour."

"I'm helping out at Kitty's rummage sale," I said, resigned to the fact that people would be surrounding me until this murder was solved.

"Oh, and one more thing. I checked the Motor Vehicle Department and I know you don't have a driver's license. If I catch you driving the truck, I'll arrest you and then I won't have to worry about where you are."

"I haven't driven for days," I lied, peering out the kitchen window at Barney's truck.

"I wasn't going to tell you I'd assigned a deputy to look out for you, but thought he might scare you if you spotted the tail."

"Thoughtful of you."

I hung up.

Cora Mae and I headed for Kitty's house in my truck for the once-in-a-lifetime mother of rummage sales. Just to be on the safe side, we were being very cautious. I bolted the door behind us, checked that all the windows were locked, and had my shotgun loaded and ready. I hoped the gun battle out at the blind proved to my attacker that I wasn't a sitting duck. If he thought he was going to easily pick off a helpless woman, he didn't know who he was messing with.

The temperature had continued to drop overnight, and a foot of new snow fell right before the cold snap hit, forming a crust of ice over the snow. Not the best day for a rummage.

The rummage sale reminded me of urban sprawl spread across Kitty's entire yard. Cars lined the road, mobs of sightseers pushed through the snow and ice, and Kitty, hunkered down in blankets, beamed from behind her shoebox of newly found cash.

"I'm using your phone," I said to her. "I forgot to do something."

I called Onni, planning to convince him that he was in danger as well.

"I'm calling to warn you that someone is trying to kill you," I said into the phone.

"The only one trying to kill me is Gertie Johnson," he said. "Who is this?"

"Er . . . this is Gertie Johnson."

"I'm going to court to get a restraining order against you. Don't ever call here again." And Onni hung up.

———

"Hi, Gert," George called, leaning against a table filled with junk, his snake hat hissing and a toothpick jutting from the side of his mouth. "This is the first rummage sale I've ever attended right after a snowstorm. Air sure is nippy."

I grunted a response.

A yellow Lab with graying fur limped over from the side of the road and wagged a crooked tail.

"Rescue dog," George told me. "I couldn't let them put him down. He's going to be my guard dog."

The dog shuffled under the table and plopped down in the snow. He yawned.

"Mean-looking cuss," I said, wondering how someone who loves animals as much as George does could do wrong by his own species. It wasn't possible.

"Heard you were over in Gladstone last night," I said casually.

George shook his head. "No. Who told you that?"

"I must have it mixed up." Wrong answer from George. I felt betrayed, anger and hurt working through my veins.

George looked at the gauze pad on my forehead. "That was a close call. How are you doing?"

Abruptly, I walked away, leaving George gaping. One more second and I would have told him what I thought of him, the creepy, lying, cheating, money-grabbing killer.

A red pickup truck cruised by and I could see a kid wearing a deputy's hat sitting behind the steering wheel. He slowed and scanned the crowd.

"Cora Mae," I said after stumbling through the snow and piles of sale items to find her. "Let's get out of here. George is following me and so is that red truck parking down the road."

Cora Mae, her arms filled with dollhouse furniture, turned and craned her neck, searching for him. "I'll stay and keep an eye on George. Make sure Kitty doesn't see you leaving alone."

I stole through the shoppers, creeping closer to my truck, careful that Kitty and George and the deputy weren't watching. I ducked down behind a row of cars and made my escape.

———

Calvin and Helen Sandberg lived on the far side of Chester's land, a mile down Rock Road. One lone dog lifted his nose to the sky in a wild howl when I drove in. He was immediately joined by dozens of other dogs staked in the yard. The symphony was brief. Then they circled their chains in unison, watching me eagerly. Those dogs knew something was up.

I'd never been to the Sandberg place before. By the looks of it, they put all their money into taking care of their dogs, which were spread out as far as the eye could see. Each one had a wood dog house with a flat roof. Some of the dogs were sitting on top of the houses. A pipe was pounded into the ground by each one with a metal swivel and a long length of chain, one end of which was attached to a dog.

I found Calvin and Helen working in the back of the dog yard and they stopped to greet me. I knew who they were from seeing them in town, but like a lot of Stonely residents, they kept to themselves.

They were in their mid-thirties and had already earned a reputation for mid-distance sled dog racing. Every year they competed in the U.P. 300 in Marquette. They had at least fifty Alaskan Huskies, and every once in a while I'd see them out on the road driving their dogs. I heard those dogs were capable of running all day without quitting.

Calvin had a gray-speckled beard that hadn't been trimmed for at least ten years. He wore a brown sock cap pulled down tight around his forehead. Helen had on a furry hat with a long raccoon tail. She kept pushing her thick glasses up on her nose while we talked.

I explained the purpose of my visit while I sized up the dogs, an ugly bunch of mutts, some with blue eyes, some with brown, and a few with one of each color. I've heard they are friendly, hard-working dogs, and I heard right because when I walked over, every tail wagged.

Suddenly the entire pack broke into a frenzy, howling and circling and straining to break loose. I jumped back and saw Calvin pulling a toboggan-sized sled over from a nearby shed. He draped a black canvas bag over the sled and began attaching it to the sled with straps.

I was dressed for cold weather, wearing my boots, my hunting cap with the earflaps down, Blue Blockers to cut the glare from the cold sun, and a pair of snowmobile gloves. I wasn't cold, but I shivered anyhow.

"Those dogs look wild to me," I said to Helen, suddenly unsure of this plan. "And . . . and . . . hairy. This might not be such a good idea. Maybe you should go for me."

"Don't worry," Calvin said. "You'll sit in the basket inside the sled bag to stay warm. All you have to do is sit there, and I'll drive you around. It'll be like a horse and buggy ride."

"That doesn't sound hard," I agreed.

"What we'll do," Calvin explained, "is cross the road onto Chester's land. There's a fairly good system of trails through there. Chester gave us permission to use his property to run our dogs and we try to keep the trails open. At least the outer set. We haven't been on the inside trails much. That's where we'll go today."

Calvin used a slipknot to tie a rope from the sled to a tree. Then he and Helen harnessed six dogs, brought them over one at a time, and hooked them up in pairs to a long rope on the front of the sled. All fifty of the dogs in the yard were barking and howling an awful racket, and the harnessed dogs were keyed up.

I crawled into the sled basket and settled in the sled bag. The dogs were frenzied to go and yanking at the lines. I glanced at the rope wrapped around the tree, nervous that it might give out or work loose, but it seemed to be holding the dogs back.

I thought I heard Calvin call to me to release the rope holding the sled. I reached over and pulled the cord, and the dogs, watching every move we made, lunged into action.

We careened down the drive, crossed the road at eighty miles an hour, soared over the ditch, and slid onto one of the trails.

I couldn't help noticing that Calvin wasn't behind me in the driver's seat.

The dogs didn't seem to care, or maybe they liked it. Less weight to haul. I chanced a quick look back and could see Calvin and Helen running and waving their arms, quickly becoming black dots in the white snow.

We charged ahead, the dogs settling into a steady sixty or seventy miles an hour. I tried to look around as we ran, but everything seemed to be a speed blur. The sled wasn't tracking nice and steady behind the dogs like you'd imagine. Instead it swerved from one side of the path to the other, hitting every rut and bump in the road.

"Gee," I called to the dogs, remembering the word but not the meaning from watching *Wide World of Sports*. I tried yelling "stop," but they didn't even hesitate. We took a soft right curve at the next intersection and began following a less worn path. Forced to work harder, the dogs slowed to a brisk trot, giving me time to assess my situation. I noticed a large claw hook in the basket next to me tied to a rope attached to the sled.

I picked up the hook and whipped it at the next small tree we passed, hoping it would anchor around the tree and stop the sled. The tree bent in half and the hook came free. I tried the same thing several more times without any luck.

"Whoa," I shrieked. Not one dog looked back. Not one seemed about to stop. They were on a mission dead ahead, and nothing was going to stop them. We were going to run all day.

Taking time to rest from throwing the hook, I looked forward just in time to see Bear Creek in front of us and a sharp turn in the path directly ahead. The dogs took the turn, the sled bounced on the shoulder of the curve, and I flew out.

I pulled my face out of the snow just in time to see the dogs disappear around another bend, dragging the sled on its side. I dropped my head on an arm and tried to catch my breath. I sat up slowly, working each leg and arm bone, but nothing appeared to be broken.

Slowly, I straightened up and looked at the frozen creek. Rocks jutted out of the ice, a sign that this section was shallow. A brisk wind traveled across the creek, sweeping the snow to the banks and stinging my eyes. I walked out onto the ice, hearing nothing but the wind, seeing nothing but swirling snow, feeling nothing but aching coldness.

The dogs had vanished and I would have to follow the creek or the path back. The creek and its secrets had drawn me here, but the path would take me back to the warmth of my truck.

It was bitter cold by now, a weather fact I hadn't noticed while on my wild ride. There's something about fear that keeps you toasty warm. I wasn't too cold except for my face, which had taken the snow wash. The wind stung like an angry swarm of wasps. The gauze bandage on my forehead came loose and dangled over one eye. I pulled it loose and dabbed it on my wound. No blood.

A voice floated on the wind and soon I could see a sled and team heading my way. This one had a driver.

"You okay?" Calvin asked when he pulled up, real concern in his voice.

"I'm okay, but what about your dogs?"

"They'll make a loop and probably be waiting for us at home. They know their way around in here."

"I thought you told me to pull the rope loose. It would have been helpful if you had been on the sled at the time."

"I said to wait until I said so and then to pull the rope."

"Rumor has it there's gold in this creek," I said, remembering what was important. "What do you think of that?"

Calvin threw out a claw hook like the one I had tried to stop the runaways with, and tromped down on the top of it, driving it into the snow. "I reckon it's a bunch of bunk, but someone thinks it's true."

"What do you mean?"

"Helen found gold panning equipment in September right over there." Calvin pointed to a spot near where I had stood on the ice. "When we get back to the house, I'll show it to you."

He jumped off and helped me roll into the sled bag. Calvin pulled the hook out of the snow, called "hike," and we were off in the direction of the runaway dogs.

Helen had already unharnessed the runaway team when we arrived. I gave the dogs fresh water while Helen went into the house and came back with a paper bag. She pulled out a green plastic pan, tweezers, and a stainless steel hand trowel.

"At first we didn't know what they were for," Calvin said. "Helen's brother told us." Calvin shook his head. "Must have been kids because no one else would believe such a thing."

"Can I borrow these?" I asked.

Helen nodded. "Why didn't you just say what you were looking for in the first place? Would have saved you a spill."

———

The six vinyl-covered tables at the Deer Horn were filled with deer hunters. I took a seat at the counter, ignoring the stunned expression on George's face when I walked right past his table.

"What ya got there?" Carl called to me. "Carryin' your bedpan with you? These are modern times. Haven't you ever heard of Depends?" All six tables of hunters turned to check out the green pan I had thrown on the counter. Laughter buzzed through the room like a chain saw slicing timber.

"Health inspector will shut me down if he sees a bedpan on my food counter." Ruthie worked the grill, glancing harshly at the pan.

"Don't worry, Ruthie, it's not a bedpan." I swirled my chair around to face the room. "Leave it to Carl to know all about adult diapers."

George leaned back casually in a chair, studying me, his eyes guarded, his expression unreadable.

I forced my own poker face, careful not to let my opponent guess what kind of hand I held. "George, you know what this is, don't you?"

"Sure, Gert, I know. What you aiming to do? Pan for gold?"

"Thought you might have lost some equipment. I'm thinking about whether to return it or not."

I thought I noticed a flicker of realization pass through his smoky eyes then it was gone. "Take your time," he said slowly. "There isn't any rush."

"You ready to take my order?" I croaked to Ruthie, swinging wildly back to the counter, a tight knot in my throat. As much as the evidence had been stacking in George's direction, I didn't really believe it until this very moment.

"Fella in Rapid River took two ounces of gold out of a gravel pit by Marquette," someone said. "That ain't much."

"Lotsa gold scammers out there to take a fool's hard-earned dollars," someone else said. "The crooks salt samples and swindle folks."

"Waitress will be right there," Ruthie said to someone at another table while she poured a cup of coffee for me. "I've heard of mining copper and iron in these parts. Gold, though . . ." She shook her head.

My daughter Star sashayed out of the kitchen, cute as a button in a frilly white waitress apron, ponytail bouncing as she walked with plates of food stacked on a tray.

"Hey, honey," I said, relieved to take my mind off George's betrayal by escaping into small talk. I kept my voice light but my hands clenching the coffee cup were white. "What you doing?"

"I'm helping Ruthie out until hunting season's over," Star said, setting the tray down and passing out plates at the table closest to the kitchen.

"How are things with the Italian Stallion?" I asked, remembering the stocky, dark guy she'd been with at the pastie dinner. "I never see you anymore."

"He's gone," Star pouted. "He was working on a special road crew, and they finished the job and moved on. I'm between men right now."

"Maybe you can find some time for me," I said. "I have my own investigation company now, and Cora Mae and Kitty help out with the legwork. Maybe when you wrap up working here you can help out, too." I raised my voice. "I have my current investigation pretty much finished up. All I have to do is drive the last few nails in."

"Sounds fun."

"And I need you to come to court with me."

"Blaze asked me, too."

"What did you say?"

"I said no, of course. I'm sticking with you. He has Heather almost convinced she should testify against you, though. Little Donny went home with some stories and she and Blaze are going back and forth on the phone about it."

I tried to remember what Little Donny could possibly tell Heather that would hurt me. There was the stun gun incident, but I was pretty sure Little Donny didn't remember. Oh, and there was the break-in at the Lampis, but we didn't take Little Donny in. I couldn't remember anything else.

By the time Star finished at the table and came around to take my order, George had disappeared from the table of hunters. At first, I thought he might have headed for the restroom, but by the time I ordered chicken noodle soup and more coffee, I realized he had slipped out of the restaurant.

With my first spoonful of soup, the restaurant door crashed open and Kitty thundered in. "You're running around loose again with no one to watch over you. I'm starting to think you don't want my protection."

"Sit down, Kitty. Lunch is on me."

That stopped her in her tracks. Nothing appeals more to Kitty than a free lunch.

"What's up?" she wanted to know, so between ordering and eating, I told her about finding the gold mining equipment and about George's admission. After that, neither of us had anything to say, each taking in the ramifications of my discoveries and my conversation with George. Kitty turned the gold pan over and studied the bottom. She set it back down.

We listened to the hunters bragging back and forth. A few were local boys, but most were from down south around Detroit and a few were from Chicago.

Times were tough, and some of the locals, needing every dollar they could scrounge up, made their land available to the out-of-towners. They flocked in, driving city cars, station wagons, and minivans, four or five guys stuffed into each one. None of them knew a thing about hunting or gun safety, and they spent a lot of time trying to kill each other, some succeeding.

They sat in places like the Deer Horn, telling lies to each other, proud that they survived without being killed, then they stuffed themselves back in their city cars and left us alone for another year.

Since hunting season was winding down with only a few days left, I guessed this group hadn't bagged a deer yet. Otherwise they'd be long gone by now. They were a scraggly bunch, unshaven and fragrant, like skunk road kill.

Not shaving or bathing is a common ritual during hunting season and I've never understood it. Some say the perfumes in shampoo and soap scare off the deer, but I can't help thinking B.O. does it better. Barney used to shower with a perfume-free soap, then dress in clothes he'd stuffed in a bag of leaves overnight. That worked great, but of course, no one went out of his way to give sound advice to these city slickers.

"We're on to something bigger than we are," Kitty finally said when her plate was empty. "Don't you think it's time to bring Blaze in, tell him what we know? He has resources we don't have."

"You're right," I agreed, reluctantly, "but I want a little more time. I'll tell him tomorrow. What's going on with your rummage sale?"

"Cora Mae's holding down the fort. We better go. I'll follow you over to my house and you can wait for me there." Kitty seemed thoughtful and distracted. "I have something I want to check out."

"You and your bedpan have a nice day now, you hear?" Carl guffawed as Kitty and I banged out the door.

————

After an afternoon nap on Kitty's couch, I double-checked my shotgun to make sure it was loaded and put loose shells in both of my jacket pockets for later. Next time George, our local killer, decided to mess with me I'd be ready to fill his rear-end with lead. For the hundredth time, I wished it was anybody but George.

A knife to my chest wouldn't have hurt much more.

The nap did me a lot of good because when I woke up I remembered that I still hadn't interviewed Onni. I had a few questions for him as well as advice on dodging bullets. And, from watching television mysteries, I knew I needed more evidence to prove my case against George.

While Cora Mae gossiped with a few rummage sale stragglers, I checked my supplies—the recharged stun gun in my purse, my weapon vest under my jacket, loaded with extra ammo for my shotgun, the pepper spray, and a Swiss army knife I had found last week in Barney's dresser drawer. Sifting through Kitty's front hall closet, I filled my arms with things I might need if I ended up outside on a surveillance mission—a facemask, hand warmers, and a fire starter. I wanted to take a flashlight but couldn't find one, settling instead on the red-handled fire starter next to the wood-burning furnace. It had a trigger like a gun, and when I pulled it, a large steady flame shot out the end. I stuffed it in my pocket.

I drove away from the warmth and comfort of my friends, wishing for the first time in a long time that I had some company next to me. But Cora Mae had to stay at the sale and Kitty was nowhere to be found. Even the scrawny deputy kid would be welcome if I could locate him.

Being a private detective is lonely work.

———

Dusk settled in as I pulled out onto the road. Winter dusk looks like an enormous rain cloud creeping in, and it comes early in the U.P. By four-thirty we start turning on our lights to get ready for another long night. I checked my watch again—almost five o'clock.

My plan was to drive over to Onni's house and convince him that George and Barb were trying to kill both of us. Once he believed me, maybe between the two of us we could work this out and devise a plan to stop them. Onni must have information that could help us.

At the four-way stop in the center of Stonely, I heard a horn blaring behind me and I saw Kitty's cousin fold out of his purple car and strut up to my window, a cigarette between his lips.

"Kitty's missing," he said, talking around the lit cigarette.

"No, she's not. I saw her a few hours ago. She said she had some checking to do."

"She's missing." He inhaled deeply and blew recycled smoke at me.

I waved it away. "How would you know? You didn't even check for her at her house because I just left there and I didn't see you."

"I got worried when she didn't call. We have a deal. Ever since she took the bodyguard job we check in with each other twice a day. She missed her check-in this afternoon. I stopped at her house a few minutes ago. No Kitty."

"She's fine," I reassured him. Cars were slowly driving around us. "I'm kind of in a hurry. If I see her, I'll tell her to call you."

"She's supposed to be guarding you. Why isn't she?"

Up ahead, I saw George pull up to the stop sign from the opposite direction and I watched him drive past us. Craning my head out the window I saw his brake lights go on and he began turning around in the road. "Gotta go," I said, and pulled away quickly.

Another horn blared behind me and George's truck appeared in my rearview mirror, gaining fast. He flicked his headlights on and off to get my attention and I hit the accelerator and roared away. He stayed with me for a while then began to fall back and eventually his lights disappeared.

When I was sure I'd safely lost George, I turned onto Onni's road, the back truck tires sliding on the road ice. I could see large patches of ice puddled across the road.

Gunning the engine, I hoped to get past the ice quick, but the truck spun out of control. The steering wheel felt like a stripped plumbing washer; it just went slack and stopped working. I tromped on the brake and that too felt disconnected from the truck. Everything went sloppy loose and there wasn't anything I could do but spin the steering wheel like a ride on a bumper car and watch the sights as they spun by.

The truck did a complete circle, then lurched toward a deep ditch, rolled over, and settled sideways in a broken patch of ditch ice.

I wasn't feeling too good. I hit my head on the top of the truck when it rolled, and I could feel a knot the size of an apple beginning to swell over my eye. I slowly moved my legs and arms and felt my ribs. Everything seemed in working order, so I reached up and forced the passenger side door open since my door was down on the ice. After climbing out, I packed snow on the top of my head to slow the swelling.

My head seemed to be taking quite a beating lately—wood splinters from the sniper attack, a nosedive into the icy-covered snow, and now this.

I moaned.

Movement took a ton of strength, and I wondered why I felt so heavy and burdened since none of my bones were broken. Then I remembered the loaded weapon vest. I thought about taking it off but didn't have the energy.

For a brief moment I wished I had listened to Blaze and worn my seatbelt. He's always preaching about seatbelts, but I come from the old days when we tucked them down deep in the seat cushions to keep them out of the way. Nobody actually wore them.

I crawled up the embankment and sat on the side of the road, assessing my situation. The temperature was dropping quickly. I guessed it must be about ten below, with the wind chill maybe thirty below. Ice crusted on my eyelashes and my hands felt cold and stiff. I couldn't remember where my hat and gloves were. I crawled back down into the truck and found my hunting hat, but didn't see my gloves, the facemask, or my purse. I crammed the hat on, flipped the earflaps down, and quickly shoved my hands into my coat pockets. I felt the fire starter deep in my pocket and thought I could warm my hands with it if worst came to worst.

Looking both ways down the road, I decided to head back to the main road, which was about a half-mile away. Onni's house was at least a mile in the opposite direction, and I didn't think I had the strength to make it that far. Feeling disoriented, I trudged down the road at a snail's pace.

Out of the twilight, I saw lights coming toward me. I squinted, hoping to recognize the driver and hoping it wasn't George. Wouldn't that be an awful end to the day? Wouldn't that be an awful end to my life?

I crept off the road, attempting to hide myself behind a telephone pole until I was sure it wasn't George. When I was sure it wasn't a truck, I bolted back into the road and waved frantically.

The car slowed and stopped and Floyd opened the door. "Good God, Gertie. What are you doing out in this weather? You'll freeze to death."

"I need help," I said, walking up. "My truck is in the ditch over there." I pointed across the road. We could barely see the truck sunk in the ditch.

"Well, git in."

I jumped into the car, the warmth from the heater blasting in my face. It felt great.

"Looks like you left the truck running and the lights are on." Floyd peered out into the night. "I'll shut everything off." He got out, crossed the road, and a few seconds later I saw the lights in the truck go out. "It's sure cold out there," he said after he climbed back into the car.

As we pulled out, I remembered my purse and stun gun were somewhere in the truck, and almost asked Floyd to turn around, but changed my mind. In another few minutes it would be completely dark and no one passing would be able to see the truck. When I got back, everything would be right where I left it.

"Thank the Lord I saw you. Passed you up in Stonely. Looked like Kitty's cousin you were talking to. You all right?" Floyd wanted to know. "You have blood all over your face."

I reached up and noticed a cut on the back of my hand. "Must be from this," I said showing him my hand.

"There's a rag in the glove compartment," he said, watching the road. "Use that. It's clean."

I wrapped my hand in the piece of cloth. The cold had pretty much stopped the bleeding anyway. It didn't look serious. I clicked on the overhead light and pulled the rearview mirror over to my side and checked out my face and head. Other than a mess of dried blood, I couldn't find any injuries other than my head knot.

My truck was in a lot worse shape than I was.

I warmed my hands next to the heat register as we drove back through Stonely. "Your house is closest," I said. "Let's stop there and I'll use your phone to call somebody to pull my truck out."

"My thoughts exactly." Floyd turned onto his road. "Come on in and warm up," he said when we pulled up to his house.

I heard a sound as I closed the car door, shrill yet muted, like a screech owl in the distance. "What's that?" I asked Floyd.

"What's what?" Floyd said, and I remembered his defective hearing aid.

"Nothing."

"I sure am glad I ran into you," Floyd said after we entered the house and he hung his coat on a hook by the door. "The good Lord guided me right to you."

"Well, that's nice, but can you guide me to your phone. I'll be out of your hair as soon as possible. Oh, look at this." I bent down and picked up a white bobby pin, the exact same kind Kitty had in her hair earlier in the day. "Has Kitty been here?"

"Say what?" Floyd had his back to me, fumbling through a kitchen drawer.

"Kitty," I said as loud as I could. "Has Kitty been here?"

"Don't know why you'd think that." Floyd turned around and grinned, not a warm friendly grin, but rather a hard, cold grimacing grin.

And I couldn't help noticing the long-bladed carving knife he held in his hand.

FOURTEEN

Word for the Day
VISCERAL (VIS uhr uhl) adj.
Intuitive; instinctive;
emotional rather than intellectual.

"WHAT ARE YOU DOING?" I asked with growing dread.

"Taking care of a few loose ends."

The first thing I did was talk myself out of collapsing on the floor. It wasn't enough that I'd almost died in a truck accident and that the knot on my head was throbbing with pain. My instinct, failing me until this moment, shouted out the truth, and it was a great measure of the importance of my friendship with George that my very first thought was of him. I muttered under my breath, "Thank you, George. Thank you for not letting me down. Thank you for not destroying my faith in humanity, my faith in you."

My gratitude was short-lived. Now was not the time to discover that Floyd's secret occupation was murderer, since I was alone with him, miles from help, and couldn't be more unprepared. I didn't have my shotgun or the stun gun, only my pepper spray.

A small voice inside told me I was probably overreacting. There must be a logical answer.

"I'm ready to go home," I said to Floyd, pretending that the knife didn't exist, that it wasn't pointing directly at me, that I wasn't up a creek without a paddle or panning equipment.

"You're going for a ride, all right," he said quietly. "But not in the direction you think."

I chose that moment to reach under my jacket, yank the pepper spray out of my vest and aim it at his face. I pressed the button. Nothing happened. The spray didn't spray and Floyd didn't fall on the ground writhing in pain like Onni had.

"The can must have frozen," I said to no one in particular, banging it against a kitchen chair while I reached into my vest with the other hand. In a blur of motion, I dropped the can, pulled out my Swiss army knife, snapped it open, and faced off with Floyd. My two-inch blade gleamed in the fluorescent kitchen light.

Floyd smirked, reached into another drawer, never taking his eyes off of me, and I found myself staring down the barrel of a gun. Floyd dropped the knife into the drawer and closed it up.

I'd used up my entire arsenal and it hadn't been enough. I raised my hands in defeat, my small knife clattering to the floor.

"Why couldn't you leave well enough alone?" Floyd's eyes had a wild, crazy gleam to them, a trait I wished I'd noticed the day I caught him in his birthday suit inside his sauna. Although, his eyes weren't my first concern at the time.

I stared at the gun. "What's happened to Kitty?" The white bobby pin lay on the floor between us where I'd dropped it attempting to defend myself.

"Wouldn't you like to know," Floyd sneered while I watched his right hand. "You two are going to meet up in the afterlife."

My mouth dropped open. "Don't tell me you killed Kitty. Why would you do that? She never harmed a flea in her whole life."

Floyd cocked the gun.

"Don't shoot me in here," I advised. "My DNA will be smeared all over the place and they'll catch you."

"Don't plan to shoot you unless you do something stupid."

"I wouldn't do anything stupid," I reassured him.

"What I am going to do is haul you out back of the garage and tie you to the clothesline pole till you freeze up good. Then I'm going to take your stiff little body and throw it in the woods back behind your truck. Everyone will think you froze to death accidentally."

"I've always had the hots for you," I said, "and you know it. Maybe you and I can blow this place together. Nobody has to know the truth."

That line always worked in the gangster movies, but it was a long shot here. I must be really desperate to even think it. If I make it out of here alive, I'll deny ever saying it.

I had to admit that the freeze-her-stiff idea was a good one, better than anything I'd ever come up with.

"Why did you kill Chester? He was your friend."

"Same reason I'm going to kill you. To protect my interests."

"You don't own the land, Floyd. You don't own the mineral rights. You don't have any rights at all."

Floyd's face flushed red, his eyes bulging, his gun hand quivering. "All I ever wanted was the land to stay the way it was. But, no, Chester wanted to sell out to a big city outfit and he wouldn't listen to sense. When I stopped by his place to see if he wanted to take a sauna and I saw the contract lying on the kitchen table, I couldn't believe it. I went out to the blind and tried to reason with him, but I couldn't talk him out of it. I didn't have a choice."

"So you went back to his house, took his rifle, and shot him?"

"I guess I panicked and wasn't thinking right. I drove off with the rifle and had to figure out how to get it back in. Would have worked out if you hadn't stuck your big nose in. And then I found out from Onni that you owned the mineral rights."

"But I didn't register the deed."

"That's right, and you never are going to have the opportunity, either."

"You don't have to kill me," I said, grasping for straws. "I won't tell anybody. I'll listen to reason. I'm not like Chester. I won't register it. In fact, I'll turn it over to you."

"You're a nosy busybody who causes trouble wherever you go. And I don't want the deed. I told you, all I want is for things to stay just the way they are."

Floyd looked rabid, hunks of spittle shot from his mouth.

I never in my wildest nightmare imagined I'd be confronting Chester's killer alone and in the dark. I thought it would be in the light of day and with a posse to back me up, with the whole place cordoned off.

My mind was telling me this was a good time to panic. Start screaming and running around. Go over the deep end. My mind and I talked back and forth, reasoning it out, and I decided the only way I had a chance was if I started thinking.

"Why, Floyd? Why do you care about Chester's land?" I asked.

"Gold," he whispered.

"That's ridiculous. There isn't any gold back there."

"In the beginning it was just a joke." Floyd's eyes glazed over and his trigger hand shook. "We were stationed in Korea, Chester, Onni, and I, and we told stories to keep our minds off of the war. Chester already owned the land, but Onni didn't hold it against him. And Onni told us about the rumor of gold and we imagined panning for gold after the war. It was all in fun, you see. Didn't think about it again for years. Then my Eva took sick and I was desperate to take care of her, and we didn't have much money. They were going to put her in a state-owned nursing home. You ever been in one of those?"

I shook my head.

"Well, I remembered what Onni said, and with God's help, I went back to Bear Creek and the Lord provided. Onni and Chester were fools not to believe it. How else could I afford to take good care of Eva?"

"You mean, you really found gold?"

"Enough to get by. Enough to put her in a good place."

I shook my head in wonder.

Then I threw the pepper spray can in Floyd's face. He raised an arm to deflect the can and he fired a wild shot as I pelted him with the fire starter from my pocket, then a bookend from the table next to me. The heavy bookend connecting with his broad forehead and the inaccuracy of his next frantic shot gave me the few precious seconds I needed to escape out the door.

I hit the driveway running, wishing I'd worn running sneakers instead of boots. They felt like they weighed fifty pounds each. By the time I reached the cover of the side of the garage, I was walking pretty slowly because the wind was engaged in a full frontal attack. I couldn't feel my hands anymore, and the cold reached into my lungs, freezing them up, too.

A shrill whistle pierced the wind, and I realized the sound came from Floyd's sauna on the far side of the house.

"Gertie," Floyd called from the porch. "Come in here right now or I'm burning the sauna. And guess who's inside?"

I remembered the rope whistles we bought on our excursion to Escanaba. Kitty was locked in the sauna, blowing on her whistle.

"I'll burn Kitty," he shouted again. I peeked around the side of the garage and saw him framed in the light from the house holding the fire starter I had thrown at his head. He had the gun in the other hand and a can of gasoline at his feet, and he looked wildly desperate.

The whistle screeched.

I hesitated. How could I run into the icy night and leave Kitty behind? Could I even find help before I froze? My eyes teared from the cold and I blinked several times to clear my vision.

Floyd began pouring fuel on the front of the sauna.

I crept around the back of the garage and plowed into the back-end of Kitty's car. Floyd must have pulled the car off the driveway to hide it from view.

Smoke swirled in the air. I smelled burning wood.

I opened the door and the buzzer went off, telling me that the keys were still in the ignition. I slipped in as quickly as possible, hoping Floyd's hearing was poor enough to miss the sound.

"Surrender," Floyd screamed over the frantic wail of the whistle and the screaming wind. "Or she dies."

Kitty's car leapt from the shadows and I bore down on the sauna. Flames licked out from the doorframe, completely covering the front of the building. Floyd saw me coming and ran toward the car, pointing his gun at the windshield.

I didn't let up. Floyd, his face frozen in shock, flung himself at the hood of the car, rolling and crashing into the windshield as I carried him with me into the wood frame of the sauna.

The sauna buckled. I threw the car in reverse, backed out, and screeched to a halt. Floyd rolled off the car groaning, his leg at an unnatural angle. I leapt from the car, kicked the gun out of his reach and continued on, running into the flaming building.

Kitty and I collided and I started to fall, but she grabbed me with one beefy arm and dragged me out with her through the gaping hole.

"I blew on that whistle till I thought my brains would ooze out," she said between sputters and coughs. "What took you so long?"

The best thing about my friends is the level of gratitude they display whenever I help them out.

———

Before we could decide whether to leave Floyd on the ground to freeze to death or to make a call and save him, Blaze screeched into the driveway with George and Cora Mae beside him.

Blaze called an ambulance after throwing a blanket over Floyd, who had stopped moaning. I wanted to straighten out his leg for him and see how loud he could scream, but I restrained myself and told my story instead.

After the ambulance crew loaded Floyd and Blaze had made arrangements for a deputy to meet the ambulance at the hospital, Kitty and I followed Blaze's sheriff's truck to his mobile home. Mary waited with hot cocoa and warm blankets. We all piled in—Blaze, George, Cora Mae, Kitty, and me.

"I suspected Floyd had killed Chester all along," Kitty said, black smudges from the fire blotting her face. "Kid in a private college out east, big satellite dish in the yard, wife in a private nursing home. It didn't add up. When George told me the gold pan belonged to Floyd, I knew for sure."

I glanced at George. "I thought it belonged to you."

George shook his head. "I saw it in Floyd's car when he stalled out last summer and I gave him a jump."

"You even said it belonged to you."

"You sure have been acting strange," George said.

"I've been acting strange? You were the one who said you owned it."

"I would have told you who owned it if you'd asked me outright. I thought we were talking code or something."

George is a fine man, but he's still a man, and their logic escapes me. I opened my mouth to try to make my point again.

Kitty interrupted. "George is the one who told Floyd he was picking you up for cards the night your house was searched. That's how Floyd knew you weren't home."

"When did you two have this enlightening discussion?" I wanted to know.

"Outside the restaurant right after you found the gold pan." Kitty slurped cocoa. "Don't you two ever talk?"

"Not since you convinced me he was trying to kill me."

George and I exchanged stares and I shrugged as if to say, sorry about that. George grinned. "That's why you've been running away from me like I'm a rabid skunk."

"Well, I was wrong," Kitty said when I glared at her. "Can't I be wrong once in a while?"

"Why did you tell me you weren't in Gladstone when we followed you. . . ." I stopped and covered my mouth.

"You've been following me?" George had a gleam in his eyes.

I felt embarrassment coloring my face. "Maybe once. Just once."

"Carl's driving a rental car while his is in for repair. We swapped vehicles so I could watch Cora Mae's house without anyone spotting me. You must have been following Carl."

Cora Mae sat at the kitchen table, not saying a word, and I noticed tears welling in her eyes. "What's up?" I asked.

"To think I almost lost both of you." She jumped up and after a round of hugs we settled back in and Cora Mae wiped her eyes.

"Everything happened at once," she said. "I closed up the sale and right after that George stopped by concerned about Gertie. Kitty was missing. Now Gertie was missing, too. We called Onni and he said that Barb and Floyd had both tried to buy the mineral rights and when Floyd found out Onni didn't have them anymore, he blew up. Onni said Floyd always had a short fuse, even in the Marines."

"We called Blaze right away," Cora Mae sniffled.

"Let's go out tomorrow," George said to me, right in front of everybody. "Now that I've been cleared of all charges against me."

I blushed for the first time in years, feeling awkward and shy. "We can talk about it later," I said, not sure I was ready, but not ready to say no to him either. He took my hand and squeezed in understanding.

"Sure," George said. "Take your time. There isn't any rush."

I looked over at Blaze. "Now we can forget about this court stuff. Right?"

Blaze wasn't nearly as understanding.

FIFTEEN

Word for the Day
IMPUGN (im PYOON) v.
Attack by argument or criticism;
oppose or challenge as false or questionable.

I MADE A FEW concessions for court. Instead of my hunting jacket and boots, I wore a black skirt, a crisp button-down white blouse, and a pair of old penny loafers I found in the back of my closet. The alternative would have been worse—Cora Mae wanted to dress me.

I thought Blaze would give up this ridiculous hearing after I almost single-handedly brought in a deranged killer and saved Kitty's life, but he dug in his heels and wouldn't budge.

He claimed all I single-handedly did was mess up and come close to getting myself killed. Maybe there were a few things I could have done differently, but Chester's murder might have gone un-solved if it wasn't for my efforts.

Blaze continued to insist that I haven't been myself since Barney died and that I needed supervision. Of course I wasn't the same—none of us were the same after Barney died. I like to think I'm a better person than I used to be.

The first thing I did after Floyd's arrest proved I still have my wits about me. I ripped up the deeded rights to the minerals on Chester's land. Bill and Onni worked out an agreement to share in the proceeds from any gold found on the land, which, they discovered through a survey, didn't amount to a whole lot. They'd never be rich, but their lives would improve.

Blaze's spiffy lawyers sat stiffly next to him in the courtroom. I took my table alone with my friends right behind me. Cora Mae, Kitty, and Star sat in a trim line.

Kitty leaned forward and whispered to me. "Impugn their case. You can do it." And she patted me on the shoulder.

I don't know how she's figuring out what my word for the day is. She must be sneaking a peek at the scrap of paper I write them on. It's the only explanation. From now on, I'm committing them to memory.

The judge wasn't too happy with me for ignoring his advice about legal counsel. After complaining about it, he read the letter from the psychological evaluator. It blah-blahed along, with the final paragraph saying it all. "While Mrs. Johnson tends to be unorthodox in her methods and eccentric in her behavior, I saw no signs of incompetence as defined by the laws of our state."

My fans clapped and shouted until the judge threatened to remove them.

Heather, my disloyal daughter from Milwaukee, was a witness for the other side.

"She's always been like this," Heather stated. "So what's the big deal now?"

Apparently, as it was explained to me later, that comment helped our side a lot. I could tell Blaze wasn't happy with Heather's testimony when he dropped his face into both hands.

I told the judge about the murder and how I had saved Kitty. I told him I had spray-painted Blaze's truck and I had bored screws into his hall floor out of love and caring. And finally, I showed him a brand new savings book from the Escanaba bank where I had returned my money after digging it up. I even let him see the balance.

The judge cleared his throat and began. "Mrs. Johnson is not incompetent simply because she knowingly chooses to do things most of us would consider foolish. We all have the right to make mistakes. Mrs. Johnson just makes more than her fair share."

He glared at the opposing side.

"Anyone," he continued, "who takes on her own case without legal representation and argues it as effectively as Mrs. Johnson has can't possibly be incompetent to manage her own affairs."

"Guardianship denied." He slammed his gavel on the bench.

My fans went wild.

———

Grandma Johnson was waiting in my living room, A large suitcase next to her chair.

"Where you been? I've been sitting here pretty near all day. And look at this place. What a dump!"

I eyed the suitcase. "Who brought you over?"

"I called George for a ride. Don't know where my family is half the time. Avoiding me as usual. Nobody's answering their phone. Nobody's home at Blaze's. Star's gone. Someone said Heather's in town visiting and she hasn't even stopped by. Everybody's forgetting about me again."

I plopped down on the couch and peeled off the penny loafers.

"What you all dressed up for? It's not like you to look decent for a change."

"What's the suitcase for?" Maybe Grandma Johnson is finally packing it in and checking into a nursing home. Hurray. No more going over there to help clean or to make her meals.

"I'm movin' in with you."

I almost swallowed my tongue.

"It's only temporary to see how I like it."

I pried my tongue out of my tonsils. "You sure you want to give up your freedom?" I stammered.

"All's I'm giving up is loneliness, if you ask me. And if you ask me, this place needs some work. You git a bucket of hot water and we'll scrub up the spare bedroom so I can stand to sleep in it. And hurry up about it."

At ninety-two, Grandma Johnson still has a lot of vinegar left in her. If you ask me.

The right side of my face started twitching.

RECIPES

Here are some of Gertie's favorite recipes for hungry hunters . . .

KITTY'S FRIED DOUGHNUTS

Finns and Swedes love their bakery. A cup of strong coffee and a doughnut will make them happy all day long. Kitty has been known to carry these around in her purse in case she gets hungry later. The secret to perfect doughnuts is the mashed potato.

Don't forget to dunk them in coffee.

Makes a bunch
   5 cups white flour
   4 tsp baking powder
   1 tsp baking soda
   1½ tsp salt
   ½ tsp cinnamon
   1 cup mashed potatoes
   1½ cups sugar

2 eggs
¼ cup melted butter
1 cup buttermilk
1 tsp vanilla
½ tsp grated lemon rind
oil for frying
powdered sugar or granulated sugar
cinnamon (optional)

Sift together flour, baking powder, baking soda, salt, and cinnamon. Add mashed potatoes and sugar. Mix well. Blend in eggs and melted butter. In separate bowl, combine buttermilk, vanilla, and lemon rind. Add to flour mix, blend well, cover, and let stand for 15 minutes.

Roll out dough and cut with doughnut cutter. Fry in oil in pan or in a deep fryer until golden brown; turn with fork, brown other side. Remove; lay on paper towel to drain and cool. Shake doughnuts in bag with granulated sugar or powdered sugar. Try ½ cup powdered sugar and 1 tsp cinnamon for a special treat. Serve warm.

GRANDMA JOHNSON'S RUTABAGA CASSEROLE

The rutabaga is a hybrid cross between a cabbage and a turnip. The Swedes, who raised bushels of potatoes, began experimenting with growing rutabagas and tried preparing them like potatoes—boiled, mashed, and treated with cream and sugar. It was an instant success. If you find the taste too strong, you can mix them with potatoes (one-third potato to two-thirds rutabaga).

Serves 4–6

    4 pounds rutabaga
    ½ cup cream (half and half)
    6 tablespoons butter
    1 tsp nutmeg
    8 tablespoons brown sugar
    1 tsp salt
    ½ tsp pepper

Peel and cut rutabaga into 1 inch cubes. Cover and boil for 20 minutes or until very tender. Drain. Combine with all other ingredients and mash until all lumps disappear.

PERFECT PUMPKIN PIE

We have contests in the U.P. to see who can grow the biggest pumpkin. I never even try to win because I like to eat my pumpkins, and those giants aren't the eating kind. Pie pumpkins are small and plump and have plenty of pulp on the inside for making pie. If you are lucky enough to use fresh pumpkin, prepare it by cutting it in chunks and steaming it 10 or 15 minutes until soft. Mash with potato masher.

1 pie
    1 9-inch deep dish pie shell
    15-ounce can pumpkin or 2 cups fresh
    14-ounce can sweetened condensed milk
    2 eggs
    1 tsp cinnamon
    ½ tsp each—ground ginger, ground nutmeg, salt
    ¼ tsp ground cloves

Preheat oven to 425 degrees. Beat pumpkin, milk, eggs, spices, and salt. Pour into crust and bake 15 minutes. Reduce heat to 350 degrees and bake another 40 minutes or until toothpick comes out clean. Cool. Serve warm or room temperature, with vanilla ice cream or whipped cream.

ABOUT THE AUTHOR

Deb Baker grew up in the Michigan Upper Peninsula with the Finns and Swedes portrayed in *Murder Passes the Buck*. She has an intimate knowledge of the life and people of the region.

She is a member of Sisters in Crime, Mystery Writers of America, and the International Sled Dog Association, where she actively races sled dogs. Her short stories have appeared in numerous literary journals, including *Passages North* and *Room of One's Own*.

Read on for an excerpt from the next
Yooper Mystery by Deb Baker

Murder Grins & Bears It

COMING SOON FROM MIDNIGHT INK

ONE

I WASN'T SURPRISED WHEN they hauled the first human body out of the back woods by mid afternoon on Monday, day three of the season.

That's bear hunting season and it started in September in the Michigan Upper Peninsula, but hunters scampered around in the woods long before that, setting bait piles, and hoping for one good illegal shot. Once they had the official go-ahead to start blasting, nothing could hold them back.

As usual I wasn't around when the body was discovered. Remembering back, I think I heard the shot first thing this morning.

I missed the action because I was busy stealing my grandson's car. His white Ford Escort had a stick shift and an extra pedal on the floor, which threw me for a loop since I've only been driving a few months and was teaching myself on a vehicle with an automatic transmission. My behind-the-wheel practice had been on hold ever since I totaled my truck.

My best friend, Cora Mae, was sitting in the passenger seat while I was trying to keep the Escort running, but it hopped around the yard like a jackrabbit. That's when I heard the shot. At the time, though, I thought it was the car backfiring or maybe the gears grinding.

My name is Gertie Johnson and I'm a recent widow. Cora Mae says because two years have passed since Barney died, I shouldn't tell people that, but I say I'll stop when I'm good and ready. Cora Mae says sixty-six years old is too young to lose interest in life. She's the expert since she buried three husbands.

I have to admit, the police scanner she gave me last year sure helped put the pink back in my cheeks.

Listening to my scanner is better than watching soap operas because it's real life and I know most of the names coming across the air waves. I'm right in the thick of things where I like to be, and that's why I was stealing the car.

It's all part of my plans for my new detective business.

Little Donny, my Milwaukee grandson, came in late last night clutching the bear hunting license he'd won in the Michigan bear lottery. He was driving his old Ford Escort with a bad muffler, so he woke up everybody in Stonely coming into town, including me, after I'd specifically warned him to slip into the house quietly.

I needed transportation today, so before Cora Mae came over Carl Anderson showed up at my house bright and early for a quick cup of coffee. He was headed into the woods to hunt.

I formulated a plan right on the spot.

It would appear simpler to have Little Donny drive me, but I've learned the hard way that, in the long run, life is easier when family members aren't involved in every little thing I do. They tend to accidentally botch my plans or they misunderstand my intentions and get all bent out of shape and try to stop me.

Like the time Blaze thought I'd lost my savings and tried to prove in a court of law that I was incompetent to manage my own affairs. He came out of that one looking really bad. Or the time Little Donny blew my cover when I was on a surveillance mission. It just doesn't pay to confide in family.

It would have been simpler still if I hadn't totaled my truck, or if Cora Mae would take up driving. I'm sick and tired of begging rides and explaining my business to everyone, especially Blaze, my interfering son, who also happens to be the local sheriff.

Blaze and I have always butted heads. I'm a go-getter and he's a sit-downer, and that bothers him more than it does me. Plus, he still gets worked up about his name. His sisters, Heather and Star, don't mind being named for the horses I never had. They think it's cute and so do I.

For some reason Blaze doesn't agree.

After starting a fresh pot of coffee, I had Carl help me haul Little Donny out of bed, which isn't the easiest thing in the world, considering Little Donny must weigh a good two hundred and eighty pounds, and hauling is really what we had to do. A beached whale would have been easier to tackle.

Nineteen-year-olds are like growing babies, testing the world and making all kinds of mistakes, and Little Donny would sleep till noon if I let him. Last night he could hardly wait to get into the woods and do some hunting. This morning, all he cares about is whatever dream put that silly smile on his face right before we woke him up.

After Carl and I prodded and poked him, he opened one eye, held his arm up to check the time on his watch, and groaned. "It's only five-thirty, Granny. Leave me alone."

"You're in Michigan now," I reminded him. "It's six-thirty here and half the day's gone." I pulled the pillow out from under him. His head bounced a few times, then he flipped onto his right side and closed his eyes.

When I realized he wasn't going to cooperate on his own, I dug under the covers at the foot of the bed and hauled one beefy leg over the side. Carl helped me finish rolling him out. We dragged him over to the kitchen table in his boxer underwear with the pictures of footballs on them and started pumping coffee into him.

Little Donny and Carl did some deer hunting together last fall, and even though Carl's closer to my age than my grandson's, they became fast friends. They stayed friends even after Little Donny loaded a buck into Carl's brand new station wagon and then discovered it wasn't dead. The inside of Carl's wagon was shredded like coleslaw by the time he got the buck out, and Little Donny didn't look so good either.

But Carl doesn't hold it against Little Donny. It takes a lot to ruffle Carl's feathers. Which reminded me of something.

"Here's the can of chicken grease you wanted," I said, pulling the two-pound coffee can from the refrigerator and placing it on the table.

Carl opened the lid and poked the congealed chicken fat with one finger. "It's hard as a rock," he said. "Why'd you store it in the fridge?" He handed it back. "Put it on the stove burner for a few minutes to soften it up, but don't let it get too hot. Don't want to burn myself."

I fired up the gas and moved the can over to the burner.

"I'm finally gonna get my bear this year, Gertie." Carl poured more coffee and leaned back so the front legs of the chair were off the floor, which drives me crazy. Teetering like that was nothing but a fall waiting to happen, and it had happened plenty over the years. You think they'd learn.

"Bears love chickens," he continued. "I know that because every time they've raided my garbage, it's right after we had chicken for supper and had throwed away the bones."

"They sure do love chicken," I agreed. "They love pigs, too. Remember the time Old Ben tried to raise pigs?"

Carl laughed.

Old Ben bought six little piglets in Escanaba, and before the end of the month none were left. Pigs and chickens are considered bear snacks and don't last long in the Upper Peninsula, or the U.P. as we call it.

Little Donny had one eye open after his first cup of coffee. I poured him another.

"There's an orange shirt in the closet for you," I said. "Go put it on."

Little Donny grumbled off to the bedroom, clutching his coffee cup, his hair standing up straight on one side of his head like he'd ironed it that way.

"Lick your hair down while you're at it," I called after him. "And hurry." I had to get him out of my way before I could put my plan in motion.

"Gonna smear that chicken grease all over myself." Carl had a smug look on his face like he was Einstein discussing an important new relativity theory. "That way when I move around from bait pile to bait pile they'll pick up my scent and follow me right over. Don't tell nobody. It's my secret ingredient."

That's got to be the dumbest idea Carl's had in a long time, but I didn't say so. The Finns and Swedes are dominant in this part of the U.P., and after you live with them for a while you notice they're a proud bunch. You don't call them dumb right to their faces. You wait until they actually do the dumb thing, then you tell everybody in town and they help you rub it in forever.

And Carl's as Swedish as it gets so he's done his own share of teasing.

Instead I tried to redirect him. "I think there's some bear magnet spray in the closet that Barney used to use. You can spray some of that on the ground. Barney swore by it."

Carl shook his head. "I tried that spray and it didn't work at all. This is my own special formula and once I prove how good it works, I'm gonna sell it out of the trunk of my car next year and get rich. Just you wait and see."

"Hope you've got your rifle scope sighted in," I said. "You don't want to miss when that bears hurtles at you because you get only one shot. Miss and you're bear lunch."

Carl rose from the table, stirred the chicken grease with a spoon, and turned off the burner. "I'm bow and arrow hunting. Got myself some new arrows, ends are sharp like razor blades."

I gaped in astonishment. Anyone who smears chicken grease all over himself and goes bear hunting with a bow and arrow either has a death wish or is plain stupid.

During gun season for bears there's no law against bow and arrow hunting like there is during deer hunting season, but there should be. Whoever made up the bear rules must have been pounding back shots of brandy while he wrote them. Plus, bow and arrow hunters are exempt from the hunter orange rule, and they run around out in the brush in camouflage. There isn't as much traffic in the woods as during deer season, but I think it's always risky to be out in camo with rifles going off.

Carl had a lot going against him. If he survived the bear attack, someone with a firearm would finish him off. The best thing that could have happened to Carl would have been losing the bear lottery in June.

"Why don't you wait till archery season to play with your bow and arrow?"

"That's three weeks away. All the bear will be shot up by then."

"Better take Little Donny along with his rifle for backup," I suggested, implementing my plan to get Little Donny out of the way.

"Sure. He already knows that I get first shot with my arrow. If I miss then he gets a go-around."

Little Donny shuffled out of the bedroom wearing the orange shirt I'd bought for him on sale in Escanaba. I'd bought the same for myself plus a pair of orange suspender pants and a new pair of running shoes. Not that I run anywhere these days. They're just comfortable, and they put a little forward spring in my step.

Although a lot of women in this part of the country hunt, I don't, but I still need orange clothes for traipsing around in the woods. Those hunters shoot at anything that moves.

"You don't have time for breakfast," I said to Little Donny when he opened the refrigerator door and bent down to peer inside.

"I have about thirty pounds of day-old bakery in the car," Carl said. "Bear bait. You can eat some of that."

Little Donny perked right up, plopped Barney's old orange ball cap with Budweiser printed across the front on his head and followed Carl and his coffee can of chicken grease out the door.

"Stay away from Carl's can of chicken grease," I called out to Little Donny. I didn't want my favorite grandson disguising himself as a chicken and getting mauled by a bear.

About time, I thought when they pulled out of the driveway in Carl's station wagon. I rushed through the house, grabbing my Blue Blocker sunglasses and oversized purse from the dresser. After rummaging through Little Donny's suitcase and clothes, I pulled his car keys out of his jacket, which was on the floor next to his bed. I sighed in relief. If the keys had been in the pants he was wearing right now, I'd have been dead in the water.

At seven-thirty I tried to start Little Donny's car and worked on it for fifteen minutes before calling up Cora Mae, who lives right down the road.

"If I remember right," I said into the phone, "one of your husbands used to drive a stick shift car."

"That was Earl," Cora Mae said, eating something crunchy into the phone.

"By any chance, did you pay attention to how he did it?"

"Did what?" Cora Mae sounded puzzled. She starts out slow in the morning but by noon she'll be sharp as a cracked bullwhip.

"Did you pay attention to how he made the car go?"

"Oh sure. He tried to teach me, but I couldn't get the hang of it. Your feet and hands have to work at the same time. It's complicated."

"But do you remember how he did it?"

"Sort of."

"I need your help," I said. "Come right over."

I waited outside impatiently until she finally strolled up the driveway. Cora Mae just turned sixty-three but she doesn't look or act her age. She had on a black, sleeveless knit top, black stretch pants, and high-heeled black sandals. The knit top was low cut and as tight as a sausage casing. Cora Mae discovered Wonderbras last year and hasn't been out of them since. Her boobs stand right up and lead the way.

"Cora Mae, can you speed it up a little?" I said. "I'm going to miss the auction."

She sashayed into the passenger seat and studied the stick shift. "That's a clutch," she said, pointing at the extra foot pedal. "You have to synchronize it with the gas." She used her hands to demonstrate. "Give it a try."

She remembered most of it. The only part she got wrong was the shifting order. After I tried to start out in fourth gear a few times and did the jackrabbit hop, she remembered it right, and we took off down the drive.

We blasted out onto the road in the stolen Ford Escort at the same time we heard the bang.

"What was that?" Cora Mae wanted to know.

"Piece of junk is backfiring," I said, grinding through the gears. "And Little Donny needs a new muffler."

———

The County auction is held annually at the Escanaba fairgrounds, forty miles down the road from Stonely. All the surrounding municipalities get together and sell stuff they don't need anymore. Last year when I still had Barney's truck, I drove over and paid only thirty dollars for a perfectly good power saw the forestry department was auctioning off.

"Where'd you get the money to bid on a truck?" Cora Mae asked on the way over. "I thought you were trying to live on your social security."

"I've got resources," I hedged.

"You dug up your money box, didn't you?"

I nodded. "It's for a good cause."

After Barney died, I went to the bank and withdrew every last penny of our money and buried it in a waterproof steel box under the apple tree. It's my future insurance against failing banks and an untrustworthy government.

I had to put it all back in the bank to beat Blaze in court, but that was only a temporary arrangement.

My pants' pockets were stuffed with wadded greenbacks, but I intended to hang on to as many as possible.

I dropped Cora Mae and her high heels at the main gate and parked Little Donny's Escort on the side of the road about three blocks from the fairgrounds, hoping nobody would park close by. If I had to use reverse, I was in real trouble.

We were just in time for the car part of the auction, and Blaze's old sheriff's truck was the first vehicle on the block.

"Now, I know this truck don't look like much," the auctioneer hollered while the crowd hooted and roared with laughter, "but it sure can run. Only a hundred thousand miles on it, and a hundred left to go."

You could hardly hear him over the howling going on.

"What happened to it?" yelled a fat heckler with a skull and crossbones tattooed on his arm. "Looks like some clown spray-painted it yellow. Look, they even spray-painted the door handle and all the trim."

The crowd roared. I was beginning to get annoyed, especially after the clown remark. I took it personally since I was the one who tried to snazzy up Blaze's rust bucket with a little new paint. I did it to help him out and never got a thank you for it.

In hindsight, I do have to admit spray paint isn't the best way to touch up a paint job. The paint ran in streaks in some spots and it was real hard to keep off the windows. That's why I went ahead and sprayed the trim. Paint was on the chrome already anyway.

"Better haul this one off to the junkyard," some other wit in the crowd shouted.

I glanced at the truck. It still had the lights and siren on the roof and I was going to need that. Someone had peeled off the Sheriff Department sign but you could still read what it said since it was a different color than the yellow I had spray-painted on.

"Five hundred dollars," I called out. "I'll give you five hundred for it."

The auctioneer's head swung in my direction. "We're starting the bidding out at eight hundred. That's rock bottom."

"Then I'm bidding rock bottom," I said.

Rock bottom went once, twice, three times and was sold to the little red-haired lady in the orange suspender pants.

That was me.

I grinned to beat the band.

———

"How are we going to get both your new truck and Little Donny's car home?" Cora Mae wanted to know.

"The truck is an automatic. You'll be able to drive it," I said. "I'll drive Little Donny's car with the stick shift and you can follow me in the truck."

"But I never renewed my driver's license. I don't have one."

"Neither do I, but in case you haven't noticed, I drive just fine." Which was sort of a lie. I've had a few scary moments and I've done a little damage, mostly to my own property. My first attempt at driving was in Barney's old truck, and I only drove it for about a week before I rolled it into a ditch. "There's no other way to do it, Cora Mae. You have to."

I paid up, filled out the required forms, motioned Cora Mae to hop into the passenger seat, and drove my new truck out of the side gate of the fairgrounds, around the block, and parked next to Little Donny's car. I pulled a screwdriver from the back seat of the Escort and screwed Barney's old truck plates onto my new truck.

After taking all this in without lifting a finger to help, Cora Mae slid into the driver's seat of the new business vehicle and waited for me to pull out in the Ford Escort. My grandson's car jumped and lurched onto the road. I ground the gears, the engine roared, I popped the clutch, and the car tore off.

I was going to have whiplash before I got this piece of junk back to Little Donny.

Before leaving Escanaba I pulled into the parking lot at the hardware store, with Cora Mae trailing in the yellow truck.

"I'll be right back," I yelled to her.

Moments later I came out carrying a lettering kit with sheets of black letters in different sizes.

"Let's hit it," I called to Cora Mae.

———

I saw the commotion as soon as I turned down Old Peterson Road with Cora Mae following behind. Sheriff and fire vehicles jammed the road, all trying to one-up each other by running every strobe light they had. An ambulance, off to the side of the road, was surrounded by deputies. One lane was sectioned off and guarded by a group of men I recognized as the assistant deputy volunteers Blaze had recruited when he was reelected last year. About thirty spectators had gathered.

Word in the U.P. travels faster than a skunked dog races for home. The crowd of spectators wasn't much of a crowd yet so this was fresh-breaking news.

I pulled over, careful to leave room between Little Donny's Ford Escort and the next vehicle so I had plenty of space to get out. Cora Mae parked behind me. I ran back to my new truck, opened the driver's door and reached past Cora Mae to flip the lights and siren switches. Might as well join the action. If I looked official I might be able to drive right into the middle of the commotion.

Nothing happened. I flipped the switches several more times before I gave up. "Dang," I muttered. "Nothing ever works when you need it."

Cora Mae teetered behind in her spiked heels as I elbowed my way to the front of the group.

"Gertie Johnson," I said, identifying myself to the volunteer deputy facing me. "I have clearance to move through."

"I'm sorry, but I have orders from Blaze and he says everyone stays on that side of the line." He stretched his arms out along the rope.

"I'm the sheriff's mother, do you know that?" He didn't flinch when I tried to intimidate him with my most threatening expression.

"Yes, ma'am, I know, but Blaze said nobody can pass. He didn't leave special instructions for you."

"What happened here?" I asked him sweetly, switching tactics. I scanned the crowd of officials, looking for Blaze. The volunteer, busy holding his line, didn't respond, so I turned back to the crowd. "Does anybody know what's going on?"

"Don't know," a man next to me said. He pointed off in the direction of the woods. "They carried someone out on a stretcher a little while ago. I'm guessing it was a dead body considerin' the way it was covered up head to toe with a blanket, eh."

"Dead hunter, for sure," someone said.

"Car accident," a woman offered.

"No crashed car around here," someone else said. "It's a dead hunter."

Something inside of me wanted to scream. I grabbed Cora Mae by the arm and squeezed. "Little Donny and Carl were hunting back in there," I croaked, not bothering to hide the panic in my voice. "Where's my grandson?"

"Don't even think it, Gertie. They're okay."

"Little Donny was hunting back there," I repeated, feeling flushed and dizzy. "Where is he?"

WWW.MIDNIGHTINKBOOKS.COM

From the gritty streets of New York City to sacred tombs in the Middle East, it's always midnight somewhere. Join us online at any hour for fresh new voices in mystery fiction, book club questions, author information, mystery resources, and more.

Midnight Ink promises a wild ride filled with cunning villains, conflicted heroes, hilarious hazards, mind-bending puzzles, and enough twists and turns to keep readers on the edge of their seats.

MIDNIGHT INK ORDERING INFORMATION

Order by Phone:
- Call toll-free within the U.S. and Canada at 1-888-NITEINK (1-888-648-3465)
- We accept VISA, MasterCard, and American Express

Order by Mail:
Send the full price of your order (MN residents add 7% sales tax) in U.S. funds, plus postage & handling to:

> Midnight Ink
> 2143 Wooddale Drive
> Woodbury, MN 55125-2989

Postage & Handling:

Standard (U.S., Mexico, & Canada). If your order is:
> $49.99 and under, add $3.00
> $50.00 and over, FREE STANDARD SHIPPING

AK, HI, PR: $15.00 for one book plus $1.00 for each additional book.

International Orders (airmail only):
> $16.00 for one book plus $3.00 for each additional book

Orders are processed within 2 business days. Please allow for normal shipping time. Postage and handling rates subject to change.